AMARA

THE RISE OF THE SHADOW BLOSSOMS

BOOK I

AMARA
THE RISE OF THE SHADOW BLOSSOMS

A Series by The Fikes Brothers

Published by Tinted Reality Media
134 Sawmill Rd
Saint Robert, MO 65584
Website: tintedrealitymedia.com

Ordering Information:
For order details, please contact efikes@tintedrealitybooks.com

Print ISBN: 979-8-9855651-8-8
eBook ISBN: 979-8-9855651-9-5

Printed in the United States of America

Disclaimer: This is a work of historical fiction. Names, characters, businesses, places, events, and incidents are either the products of the author's imagination or used in a fictitious manner. Any resemblance to actual persons, living or dead, or actual events is purely coincidental.

Dedication

To our grandmother, Arlena Rutledge,

For your bravery growing up in the segregated rural South, where a woman of color faced stifling constraints on her growth. Despite societal norms that sought to dim your light, you never allowed them to stop you from becoming a beacon that shone brightly throughout our family. Your rays continue to emanate, touching generations later, casting an ethereal glow on all your descendants. You were the inspiration for Amara.

And to Hapuna Beach,

Where the gentle breeze caressed my face with a comforting touch, reminiscent of my mother's hands applying lotion to my skin before school. The scent of salt in the air, mingling with the fragrance of blooming plumeria, filled my lungs with every breath. The golden sands embraced my feet with every step, softly guiding my path. The rhythmic symphony of crashing waves and the distant calls of seabirds provided a serene backdrop to my thoughts, etching memories as timeless as the shoreline. Looking out at the vast infinity of the ocean where the sky seamlessly intersects, I bear witness to your beauty. This sacred place granted me a clear and sound mind to complete this manuscript, pulling me away from the relentless notifications that clutter my phone screen, immersing me in a true state of "Focus Mode." The warmth of the sun on my skin and the gentle rustle of palm leaves overhead allowed my thoughts to flow freely, bringing this work to life.

Prologue

***

The Gift

(贈り物)

The year was 1579, and sheets of rain draped themselves over a modest, rural settlement of Midoriya, nestled within the outskirts of Japan's Suruga province. Hooves pounded the softened earth, each stride sinking deeper into the rain-soaked ground as two weary travelers sought refuge from a relentless storm.

A Jesuit missionary named Alessandro—on a mission to spread Christianity through Japan—and his stalwart bodyguard rode into the humble community. Alessandro had found success in other provinces, bringing the message of Christianity to those willing to listen. However, as of late, his efforts here had been met with fierce resistance from those who were viewing Christianity as a threat to their Buddhist traditions and way of life.

The tension was perceptible, many fearing that the religion sought to dilute or replace their centuries-old beliefs. The bodyguard, a former slave who had earned his freedom through valor and loyalty, had been tasked with protecting Alessandro from such attackers, ensuring the missionary could continue his work despite the growing danger. Their arrival, shadowed under dim and stormy skies, stirred an unusual excitement within a local merchant.

His name was Takeda Hideyoshi.

Takeda urgently led his twenty-year-old daughter, Yuki, to attend to the unexpected guests. The two figures dismounted their horses, their outlines looming large against the driving rain.

As they shrugged off their hoods, a curtain of water dripping from the brims of their headwear, the air was buzzing with whispers and speculation. Their foreign features and attire now drew the attention of every onlooker, none more so than Yuki, who found herself momentarily startled as she drew closer.

The bodyguard was a striking figure, a tall, dark-skinned African man whose presence commanded both awe and fear.

His skin, a deep ebony, contrasted sharply with the pale complexions of the Japanese and the Portuguese Jesuits. Yuki had seen Africans before, but none had ever been this close or this real.

Shaking off her surprise with a discreet grace, she led the men to the shelter of a makeshift awning, providing them with immediate relief from the relentless downpour.

Amid the comforting smell of an aromatic steamy broth, the two men gladly shed their rain-soaked garb, placing their garments near the fire to dry. Soon, steam was rising from the clothes, the dancing firelight painting the men's faces in its glow.

Tired and chilled, they gratefully accepted the nourishment Yuki was offering, relishing the allure of the freshly prepared food.

The African bodyguard, his intense stare fixed on his surroundings, couldn't help but notice Yuki's allure too.

Duty, however, cautioned him against exposing his vulnerability.

Alessandro, consulting and jabbing his map, announced, "We are here. Should the weather clear up, we can depart at dawn and should reach Owari in seven days. Otherwise, we're looking at a journey of at least a week and a half if it continues raining like this."

The African, maintaining his silence, simply nodded.

He would take the weather however it came.

The bodyguard still eyed Yuki, willing things were different, and that he could stay focused on his work. He dared not let his growing admiration for Yuki detract from his ever-vigilant guard.

Yet, unbeknownst to him, the young woman was equally intrigued, her curiosity piqued by the silent, stoic man before her. However, her culture and social standing strictly prohibited unsolicited interaction with men of any kind, even with those of foreign descent.

Yet Yuki, always one to challenge societal boundaries, was feeling a compelling curiosity about this mysterious guardian. Now and then, her young eyes rose to see what the stranger might be doing—and whether he was eyeing her too. She was undoubtedly entranced.

As the men concluded their meal, they studied a further array of maps, their edges flickering in the fire's glow.

With the storm showing no sign of letting up, Alessandro negotiated the rental of two tents from Takeda, a short-term solution to an awkward problem outside of his control. He was intending to resume their journey once the weather cleared, not wanting their horses to end up mired in the region's notorious mud-slicked valleys.

The evening fell gently and slowly, time seeming to pass at a slower pace here than when out on their travels, a welcome change.

The sunset was already draping the humble settlement in a blanket of serene tranquility. The men grabbed their overcoats, dried and warmed by the fire, and were duly ushered to their tents.

The rain softened to a murmur as darkness weaved its quiet spell into a vast night sky. Beneath the sprawling canopy of ancient trees, fireflies soon began their nocturnal dance, casting an enchanting bioluminescence across the peaceful land, a magical ambiance.

Seated on his bedroll within the confines of his temporary shelter, the bodyguard carefully tended to his sword, every stroke evidence of a warrior's solid discipline to repeat the same task each evening.

As he did so, the fleeting glow of the fireflies drew a spectral silhouette against the tent's fabric—the silhouette, in fact, of a woman. Unstartled, the bodyguard rose with ease.

He quietly stepped outside into the dimly lit night.

There, bathed in the soft luminescence of nature's light, stood Yuki, silent and mesmerizing, simply standing there.

She had approached with a basket of freshly picked fruit for the men. Language barriers were looming between them, a bridge yet to be traversed, but she stretched out her arms, offering the food. Her meaning was clear enough, yet both would have liked to speak.

Overcome by a surge of boldness uncharacteristic of his usual disciplined demeanor, the African bodyguard saw an opportunity to introduce himself formally. He smiled, standing to one side.

With a welcoming gesture, he guided her into his tent.

As they sat on his bedroll, she pointed to herself and softly uttered, "Yuki." Her look was inquisitive but also a little shy, graceful, and filled with warmth. On her face was a smile as wide as his own.

He echoed her name, a foreign sound that warmed the space between them. Then he pointed to himself and replied, "Yasufe."

Another gentle smile adorned her lips as she repeated his name, signifying the birth of a powerful connection between the two.

Yuki, her hands trembling, reached out, her fingertips tracing a tender path across Yasufe's face, seeking to familiarize herself with every contour as if she had never known skin like his before.

Her touch was an intimate gesture shimmering with curiosity and passion. As for Yasufe, he did not flinch from her fingertips either.

Yuki's heart echoed the rhythm of the fireflies in their ethereal dance outside the tent, fluttering wildly within the confines of her chest, going against everything taught to her as a traditional Japanese woman. Almost driven to this stranger by a magnetic pull, she yearned to confirm the authenticity of the connection sparking between them. The air seemed to thrum with romance, the raw energy emanating from her in invisible waves.

Yasufe responded to her touch, an electrifying undercurrent of desire surging through him at her tender caress.

As the night deepened, the outside world ceased to exist for them; they were consumed by the privacy of their shared tent.

It was in this cloistered universe, cocooned in the still of the night, that Yasufe dared to lower his carefully maintained defenses.

Under the veiled secrecy of nightfall, Yasufe and Yuki succumbed to the profound longing coursing between them. Bound by a passion as deep as it was unexpected, their bodies intertwined in a dance as ancient as time. Yielding to their shared desire's power, they made love, the night sky bearing silent witness to their intimate union.

Their connection, fostered in silence and mutual fascination, now bloomed into a passionate affair that would last until the early tendrils of dawn began to seep into the night sky.

Of course, before daylight could stake its claim on the Midoriya, Yuki stealthily retraced her steps back to her tent.

A torrent of emotions was coursing through her veins, the intensity akin to the lingering traces of the night's passion. Yasufe's touch, still a tangible memory imprinted on her skin, radiated a comforting glow now enveloping her in a cocoon of safety.

She could almost sense the solid strength of his arms still cradling her, the vestiges of their shared intimacy forming a protective shield around her. Surrendering to these sensations, Yuki let the gentle lull of her thoughts guide her into the realm of early morning slumber.

No sooner had Yuki surrendered herself to the tranquility of sleep than it seemed the gruff voice of her father was intent on rousing her again. He was calling for her to aid the men with their belongings as they readied themselves for departure.

With the storm reluctantly retreating, Alessandro had decided it was time to continue their journey.

A sharp pang of sorrow twisted within Yuki at the prospect of their departure, a dread she felt deep in her throat as she watched Yasufe burdening his horse with his luggage.

The sight left her grappling with the harsh reality that she might never again lay eyes on the intimidating yet soft-hearted warrior.

Outwardly, Yasufe bore his composed demeanor as a bodyguard's shield. Internally, however, a seed of deep affection for Yuki had already taken root. As Alessandro moved away to settle accounts with Takeda, a fleeting window of solitude was left just for the two.

Unable to hold back, Yuki rushed to Yasufe, her arms embracing him with a desperate intensity.

He responded the same way, wrapping her in his powerful arms while also striving to keep his own turbulent emotions in check.

Raindrops traced their contours as he gently took her left hand and pressed a lingering kiss to its back. He then turned to mount his horse, his dark silhouette framed against the stormy morning.

Alessandro returned at that precise moment, vaulting onto his steed, and together, they began their passage into the forest's looming embrace. As the men gradually disappeared into a rain-shrouded wilderness, Yuki stood motionless, her stare riveted on the forest's edge until they were nothing but shadows swallowed by the green.

Turning back to the dim, rain-soaked settlement, tears welled in her eyes, their journey down her cheeks concealed by the persistent drizzle. She retreated to the solitude of her tent, her heart aching with the bittersweet mixture of love and loss.

Unbeknownst to Yuki and Yasufe, however, a precious gift from their passionate union had already begun its life journey. Nestled within Yuki's womb, their love's legacy had found a place to grow.

Throughout the ensuing three years, Yasufe solidified his reputation as an indomitable warrior during Japan's turbulent Sengoku period.

He commanded and molded a potent army at the behest of the mighty feudal lord, Oda Nobunaga, an iron fist propelling Nobunaga to unify and preside over Japan.

So profound was Yasufe's contribution that Nobunaga honored him with a Japanese name, Yasuke, thereby bestowing upon him the revered samurai title, an honor unprecedented for a foreigner.

This christened Yasuke with an esteemed status, earning him the respect and admiration of all in the community he called home.

However, late 1582 brought with it fickle tides of fortune.

Like an infiltrator, treachery came creeping into Nobunaga's ranks, threatening to topple the empire he had so painstakingly built.

Trapped in a situation offering not even the faintest prospect of victory, Nobunaga staunchly refused to fall into the hands of his adversaries. He ordered Yasuke to sever his head and return it to his kin, an act intent on denying his enemies their twisted satisfaction of seeking him out and cleaving it from his shoulders, a fine trophy.

Yasuke, loyal to the bone, was prepared to brave death's door for his lord, so following Nobunaga's ritual suicide by his own blade, Yasuke, with a heavy heart, fulfilled his lord's final command.

He decapitated him.

With the enemy forces threatening to engulf Nobunaga's estate, Yasuke melted away into the enveloping darkness.

Behind him, he left a legacy shrouded in local mystery.

CHAPTER ONE

The New World

(新しい世界)

In the aftermath of Lord Oda Nobunaga's downfall, Japan plunged into a maelstrom of shifting loyalties, casting its many provinces into turmoil. With Nobunaga's death, the dominion of Owari Province succumbed to the unyielding grasp of Lord Hideaki, commander of the unstoppable Iron Hideaki Bushi.

A man of legendary bloodlust, Hideaki perpetuated a ceaseless state of war across the land. Should anyone seek to block his path, he resorted to a scorched-earth policy, reducing entire villages to smoldering ruins. Hideaki intended this calculated savagery to be a memorable message etched in flame and ash.

Its meaning was clear to anyone who might dare oppose him.

Yet it wasn't merely his ruthless tactics that left an indelible impression on the populace; his very presence was a manifestation of dread. Towering far above most men, his square jaw and hawk-like eyes also exuded an air of the most fearsome authority.

A gnarled scar, originating from his left temple and extending to his jawline, stood as a grim witness to his battle-hardened life, a perpetual mark of his merciless disposition.

"My Lord, our scouts report stout resistance in the northern villages," Yoshinori said, calm yet brimming with ambition.

Hideaki turned his piercing stare toward his son. "Resistance, you say? It seems we did not sufficiently quell the last uprising. If others feel so emboldened to resist, we must make an example of them. This time, we shall behead all the males before their women and children. Ensure the Iron Bushi are prepared to move at dawn."

"Of course, my Lord," Yoshinori replied, a cold smile on his lips. "This response will indeed serve as a warning to others. A river of blood is sufficient to deter even the most defiant."

Hideaki nodded, satisfaction gleaming in his hawk-like eyes. "Remember, Yoshinori, fear is our greatest weapon. Let them see the ruins and know their fate if they dare stand against us."

As Hideaki's chosen successor, Yoshinori was a different breed of predator, being cunning, manipulative, and notorious for his intricate web of spies and informants. In contrast to his fearsome father, Yoshinori was a strikingly handsome man who exuded tranquility despite the raging storm of ambition within him.

Though he had inherited his father's penetrating stare, his features were devoid of scars or harsh lines, offering a face far more amiable.

Gifted with an adaptive charisma, he could as easily win over the high nobility as the common folk, his eloquence making him equally at home amongst the town magistrates as in the marketplace.

Many mistook his refined demeanor for a lack of decisiveness, a fatal error since his hunger for war and dominion equaled his father's, often surpassing it. A meadow on his estate grimly spoke of this unquenchable thirst: it was here that he relished displaying the severed heads of his defeated foes, a chilling garden that grew with each victory as if nourished by the blood spilled in his name.

In a bold display of audacity, Hideaki and his son Yoshinori executed their merciless rule, all while remaining unchallenged by Shogun Tokugawa Ieyasu and the Tokugawa Shogunate.

While Tokugawa had once been a close ally of Nobunaga, his hands had been tied by direct imperial edict.

The emperor had commanded Tokugawa to refrain from intervening, swayed by the lucrative tributes amassed through the heavy taxation imposed by Hideaki and Yoshinori.

Little did Tokugawa suspect that, even as they bought the emperor's favor, both father and son harbored secret ambitions. When the time was ripe, they fully intended to overthrow him.

"My Lord, the shogun remains blind to our true intentions," Yoshinori remarked one evening as they dined in the opulent hall of Hideaki's estate. Hideaki smirked, setting down his cup of sake.

"The emperor's greed is our greatest ally. As long as we keep the tributes flowing, Tokugawa's hands remain bound. But remember, Yoshinori, patience is crucial. We must build our strength in the shadows. Only a foolish man makes haste in such a scenario."

While Lord Hideaki's oppressive taxation continued to drain the lifeblood of the Owari Province, he strategically reinvigorated his military forces. With calculating foresight, he began to import cutting-edge weapons from Portuguese traders, intertwining the destinies of distant lands with the fate of his dominion.

"These foreign weapons," Yoshinori said, examining a finely crafted matchlock pistol, "will give our bushi an undeniable advantage. The Shogunate will be ill prepared for what we will unleash against them someday."

Hideaki nodded his approval.

"Indeed. Our arsenal must be unmatched. The Portuguese see only profit, yet they unknowingly fuel our ascension."

As he settled in the fortified chambers of his estate, surrounded by the seasoned samurai of his bushi, a steady procession of traders came forth. Each one entered with trepidation and eagerness, aware that the prospect of striking a deal with the daimyo could elevate them to untold heights or plunge them into ruin.

Either way, something monumental would ensue.

With a discerning eye, Lord Hideaki scrutinized each weapon presented before him. Though he found himself drawn to a masterfully crafted crossbow that he swiftly added to his arsenal, it was a uniquely modified matchlock pistol that truly seized his imagination. He recognized its rare nature, commanding, "Have my name etched into this firearm. It shall be mine alone."

As daylight waned and shadows crept across his residence, the daimyo had either bartered for or outright purchased an impressive array of weaponry, numbering in the hundreds, for his elite bushi.

Each addition to his military arsenal sharpened the nebulous contours of his grand scheme to dominate Japan.

"My Lord, at this rate, our arsenal will grow stronger with each passing day," Yoshinori observed, his eyes gleaming with ambition.

"Indeed, Yoshinori," Hideaki replied, nodding, his eyes alight.

"These weapons will ensure our supremacy. But remember, they are just tools. It is our will and strategy that will conquer Japan."

Over the next two weeks, Lord Hideaki continuously amassed a daunting arsenal, each weapon another instrument in his fine symphony of war. Meanwhile, Yoshinori was equally busy in the training yards, diligently matching each piece of deadly steel to the bushi warrior best suited to wield it. Yet, amidst this cavalcade of modern weaponry, he refrained from claiming a weapon for his use.

"Yoshinori, why do you not take one of these fine weapons for yourself?" a fellow samurai inquired as they trained. "You do not see how they glint in the light? You do not feel a yearning to take one?"

Yoshinori, his eyes steady, chuckled sarcastically.

"I see it. I am a master of the blade. There is an undeniably intimate poetry in the sweep of steel through air, in the precise moment when an opponent's life is severed from his body."

There came a slight pause as the other samurai listened to Yoshinori's words.

"Modern weapons offer efficiency, but they lack the deep personal satisfaction of a skillful draw, a perfect cut, and a decisive beheading. The weapon does not make the skill."

He demonstrated a flawless strike, the blade slicing through the air with a whisper, proclaiming his flawless art.

"I take pride not in the machinery of death but in the ancient, honed skill connecting me to the warriors of old."

The samurai nodded, understanding the depth of Yoshinori's devotion to the art of the sword. "Indeed, your skill is unmatched, Yoshinori. The bushi are fortunate to have a leader who values tradition and innovation in such a way."

Yoshinori's eyes narrowed.

"Tradition grounds us, and innovation propels us forward. Together, we shall be unstoppable."

In the depths of one fateful night, Lord Hideaki called together an assembly with Yoshinori and the most trusted members of his bushi.

Within the dimly lit chamber, the daimyo unfurled a sprawling map across a grand table, pointing to various provinces of Japan. He jabbed his fingertip into the parchment.

"My warriors, behold the senryaku of our destiny, a new world that we shall install in phases over the next ten to fifteen years," Hideaki uttered with depth and conviction.

This cunningly new plan was devised to elude Shogun Tokugawa Ieyasu's vigilant eyes and amass more incredible wealth, with which they could appease the emperor's never-ending appetite for tribute.

Yoshinori leaned in, studying the map.

"My Lord, the shogun's spies are everywhere. Eventually, he will surely hear the whispers about our idea. How do we ensure they do not catch wind of our strategies?"

"By continuing to nurture the emperor's favor, of course," Hideaki added. "We shall acquire impunity, giving us the freedom to gradually envelop the land in our influence. Even if rumors landed on his ears, the emperor would be occupied with other obligations."

The enormity of Hideaki's arsenal had already rendered him a challenging force, yet even he was cautious not to underestimate the sprawling military might of the shogunate. Despite the revolutionary weapons at their disposal and the evolving war tactics, dismantling the shogunate was a mountainous task.

A bushi member had a question.

"Lord Hideaki, our forces are strong, but the shogunate's reach is vast. What if we face resistance from within?"

Hideaki's eyes narrowed. "This, my warriors, is why we must move like shadows. By the time Shogun Tokugawa grasps the wickedness of our scheme, we shall have garnered the loyalty of more than half the land, bringing other warriors into our fold."

Silence enveloped the chamber like a dense mist as the room absorbed the gravity of Hideaki's scheme.

Finally, it was Yoshinori who broke the stillness.

"Your plan is unparalleled in its cunning, my Lord," he said to his father with reverence. "You know my persuasion already. To conquer by stealth suits me well. Yet, I wonder, how can we accumulate the increase in wealth this endeavor demands?"

"We shall continue to tighten our fiscal grip on Owari Province," Hideaki declared. "Taxation shall swell, and new edicts shall be enacted. This will form the bedrock of our financial fortitude."

Lord Hideaki then unrolled an ornate scroll with a measured pause, presenting the detailed tenets of what he solemnly termed the 'iron fist tax.' Set to be imposed immediately, this merciless levy would brook no negotiation. Should any family fail in its timely payments, the sum would double, and the consequences for non-compliance would be dire. Either a member of the delinquent family would be conscripted into Hideaki's ever-expanding army or condemned to a life of ceaseless toil in forced labor camps.

"As you see, the iron fist tax shall ensure our coffers remain full, enabling us to contribute to our grand designs," Hideaki pronounced, glancing at his warriors, his stare finally resting on Yoshinori.

Yoshinori nodded subtly, signaling his approval of this most audacious plan. His mind was already racing with possibilities.

"My Lord, this will indeed fill our coffers, and it will also sow a great fear among the people. Even in their sleep, they will writhe and turn, their minds playing out the torment of payments due."

Hideaki felt a surge of satisfaction; his labyrinthine plans were winning his son's and warriors' endorsements. Yet, he had another card to play that outstripped the rest in its malevolence.

Lord Hideaki then unfurled the edict known as the 'daughter levy.' This vile decree would ensnare all families boasting a daughter of marriageable age, deemed to be between fourteen and twenty-five years. The levy mandated a hefty monthly tax payable in coins or grain. For those families too destitute to meet these obligations, their daughters would become forfeit.

These unfortunates would join the dismal ranks of the 'Handmaidens of Hideaki,' a hellish, cloistered community operated under the aegis of Hideaki's bushi. Within these walls, young women would be condemned to forced labor, religious indoctrination, and sexual exploitation. In effect, the new law would render it fiscally impossible for families to rear daughters as anything beyond mere household servants to be quickly married off.

In addition, through the daughter levy, Hideaki sought to subjugate women; he aimed to control the very fabric of society by deciding who could marry whom, who would get educated, and who must remain subservient, all while filling their own coffers and quashing any seeds or vague notions of rebellion.

"My Lord, this will break the spirits of many, but it will also secure our dominance," Yoshinori said, pacing thoughtfully around the grand table, his finger lightly tapping his chin.

"However, we must be prepared for the backlash. There will be those who will not take kindly to such decrees."

Not to be outdone by his father, he presented his proposal, intended to minimize the backlash.

"Honorable warriors. As you know, I have eyes and ears in every corner of our lands, spies and informants who keep us abreast of developments," he said. "I propose we give them, as well as any who offer valuable information, added incentives. Rewards such as tax exemptions or extra food rations will encourage loyalty to our cause and sow distrust among those who might oppose us."

Yoshinori paused, letting his previous proposal hang in the air.

"Furthermore, my Lord, I propose we strengthen our hold over the newly conquered provinces through a system of collateral hostages," he said with a note of dark determination. "We shall take the children of noble families into captivity. Their presence under our roof will serve as a tangible guarantee of their families' compliance and unswerving loyalty."

The council chamber was tense with the unmistakable gravity of Yoshinori and Lord Hideaki's words as each bushi pondered the chilling efficacy of the plan. The tactic, both cunning and cruel, would bind the newly conquered territories to Lord Hideaki's will, ensuring obedience through the dual bonds of blood and fear.

With these changes implemented, it was clear that Lord Hideaki and Yoshinori would not just be satisfied with mere conquest; they aimed to break the spirit of the people, reshaping society in their sinister image. The specter of war and bloodshed would be their final, irrefutable argument to enforce their draconian laws.

It wasn't long until the implementation of Lord Hideaki's master plan began to sweep through Owari Province like an unyielding tide, meeting little resistance. More than five years into this grand strategy, the Hideaki clan and its mighty bushi had triumphantly seized the Province of Mino, its choice far from arbitrary. Mino held a strategic position in Japan that could not be overlooked.

Fertile lands stretched across its region, abundant with soil and possibility. Incredibly fertile were its rice paddies.

This strategic acquisition gave Hideaki significant leverage, not merely in matters of commerce but also as a tool to fortify his military forces. Hideaki understood that food was a powerful motivator, nearly as persuasive as a sword's edge in matters of loyalty and obedience.

His strategy: by controlling the grain, you control the will of the people.

Here in Mino, they held not just land but also the seeds of power and control over a significant source of Japan's grain supply.

With calculated foresight, Yoshinori persuaded his father, Lord Hideaki, to make the newly conquered Mino province into a training ground for their elite bushi. The geography of Mino, with its plains and hills, provided an ideal setting for diverse combat scenarios.

In this land, warriors could practice open-field combat and also learn to navigate skirmishes on uneven, challenging terrain.

Beyond its physical attributes, Mino offered another benefit: seclusion. The quiet areas served as a sanctuary where Yoshinori's bushi could train with focus, honing their skills without distractions.

Moreover, the secluded environs were perfect for developing innovative tactics and strategies without any risk of espionage.

So far, Lord Hideaki's plans had unfolded without a hitch; Owari and now, Mino, were just the beginning. As Hideaki considered the future, all his aspirations seemed to be coming within reach.

Yet, he also recognized his son's evolving ingenuity, appreciating in Yoshinori a cunning strategist who knew how to turn the features of a subdued land into a weapon.

CHAPTER TWO

The Familiar Stranger

(知り合いの他人)

Six winters had descended upon the land nestled in the northern territories of Suruga province, each leaving its unique signature on the landscape. The once intimate settlement of Midoriya had evolved by now, gradually transforming into a burgeoning community.

In the faint luminescence of another nascent day, a hulking figure emerged from the forest's edge, cloaked in the mystery of the early morning fog. His rough hands were covered in mud, having just buried items in the soft ground.

The crisp scent of pine and earth clung to his worn garments, and the soft rustle of leaves accompanied his every step as he silently navigated his way toward the marketplace.

Upon reaching a weathered merchant stand, the enigmatic wanderer sought out a man named Takeda. The vendor, a young man just reaching his prime, responded to the inquiry by saying, "You have the right man. I am Takeda. What brings you to me?"

However, the stranger, his tone echoing an unmistakable note of confusion, insisted that it could not be so.

"You are far too young to be the Takeda I seek. Tell me, where is there another of the same name?"

The merchant's expression softened as he explained.

"Then you must mean my late father. He surrendered to the unforgiving clutches of the last winter." The air grew heavier with the scent of damp earth as the news lingered between them.

Breaking the stillness after a time, the stranger inquired, "And what of Yuki? Is she well? Where might I find her?" Upon hearing his sister's name, the merchant's eyes narrowed suspiciously.

"What business do you have with my sister?" he demanded.

Displaying a dispassionate exterior, the mysterious man described a memory from his past. "I have no business with her, only that she once offered sustenance and shelter under her father's instructions. I am grateful for it, and never forgot."

This revelation seemed to soften the merchant; he then went on to explain that Yuki now lived on the outskirts of the community in a desolate area called Yamazato.

"She has been cast out?" inquired the stranger, his broken Japanese tinged with curiosity.

"My sister is a shattered soul, unfit to live among us. She has always been rebellious, defying our ways. Then she committed the ultimate dishonor by bearing a child of foreign blood. The only reason she still breathes is because of our family name."

The mention of a child with foreign skin and blood stirred something deep within the stranger.

A veil of contemplation shrouded his expression.

"Regardless, I wish to express my gratitude to her for the aid she provided me years ago," the stranger said. "Please, tell me how to find her. It is the least I can do to repay her unquestioning kindness."

With a gesture as subtle as the morning breeze, the young Takeda directed the concealed stranger toward the remote direction of the community. His head tilted, wondering why a man would make such an effort to find a woman he barely knew, from so long ago.

"It is a long journey; you should procure some sustenance before you depart," he suggested regardless, pointing to the array of fruits on his stand. However, the stranger, awash with a cocktail of elation at the prospect of seeing Yuki, politely declined.

"It is more for me to carry. I prefer to travel fleet footed."

"As you wish, sir," remarked the vendor.

Concealing his emotional turmoil beneath a cloak of stoic calm, the stranger swiftly set off, his figure quickly swallowed by the soft morning light as he ventured toward the secluded area of Yamazato.

It was the heart of the afternoon in Yamazato, with cherry blossoms adorning the trees in their annual spectacle, creating a fine carpet of pink petals underfoot and scenting the air with perfume.

An energetic young girl was engrossed in her own playful subterfuge, escaping her mother's attentive calls.

"Amara, Amara," echoed her mother's voice, filled with tender admonishment. "No Manjū before your meal."

Her words were met with a mischievous giggle as the girl savored her stolen treat out of sight, a wave of contentment washing over her face at the taste of the sweet pastry.

Abruptly, the crackle of a broken twig passed through the air, signaling her mother's nearing presence. Amara bolted away, still aglow with giggles and the thrill of her small rebellion. As she risked a glance over her shoulder, her path ahead became unexpectedly obstructed by a towering figure. Unseen in her backward gaze, she collided with the stranger, sending Amara tumbling to the ground.

Shaking off the initial shock, she scrambled back to her feet, her young eyes wide with surprise and curiosity. She stared up at the tall figure, an impromptu question spilling from her lips.

"Who are you?" she asked.

The man remained silent, his stare steadfast on the young girl.

A hint of profound admiration shone in his eyes, but his lips held the silence hostage.

The imposing figure strode purposefully toward Amara, yet the young girl held her ground, her bravery still undiminished.

"Who are you? You ... you're not familiar to this place," she challenged him, her voice resonating with unwavering determination despite its youthful pitch and the diminutive stature of her age.

Oblivious to Amara's inquisitiveness, the stranger replied with a question of his own.

"How old might you be, little one?" he inquired.

"I am six, and I don't fear you," Amara declared, her young face set with fierce intent. She stood straight, staring into the man's face as if issuing a defiant challenge.

His response was a soft chuckle.

"Is that so? That's good, for I have no intention of scaring you. If I may ask, where might your parents be?" he probed further.

Amara still stood her ground. "I won't answer any more questions until you've answered mine," she declared.

"You're only six, yet so very wise," the stranger mused, his admiration clear. "Your parents have instructed you well."

A tranquil silence prevailed as the pair locked themselves in a mutual, unyielding stare, neither backing down.

The rhythm was broken by a voice calling from a distance, "Amara, Amara!" Yet, Amara, in her strong-mindedness, ignored the summons too, maintaining her fierce stare-down with the stranger.

The distant voice grew nearer until it broke the tableau. "There you are," the voice announced, belonging to a woman who briskly swept Amara away from the stranger and held her close.

"Please accept my apologies, O-kata. My daughter can be rather headstrong. We'll leave you be," the woman began.

As the mother-daughter duo prepared to retreat, a low voice from behind softly echoed, "Yuki." Upon no response, he tried again, this time louder, "Yuki-sama!" The woman halted in her tracks and turned to the man, confusion and curiosity on her face.

"Yes, do … do we know each other?"

In response, the stranger began to remove his worn-out cloaks. Each layer seemed to fall like autumn leaves, while time seemed to hold its breath. As the stranger's face came into view, Yuki squinted, her heart hammering as recognition dawned.

Finally, beneath the scruffy beard, the stranger's face was fully revealed. Amara looked up at her mother, her heart wrenching at the sight of her mother's tear-streaked face. Yuki let go of Amara's hand, her emotions heaving as she sprinted toward the stranger.

"Yasufe!" she cried, her voice echoing around them.

"Yasufe!" Each tear she shed landed on the ground, marking each step of her approach.

Now fully revealed, the stranger let a smile transform his once-phlegmatic face. As Yuki neared, he reached out, his robust hands enveloping her in a tight embrace, each second of the hug trying to compensate for years of lost time.

"Yuki, it's been a long time," Yasufe said softly as his calloused hands caressed her hair. He spoke in a whisper.

"Yes, the years have been hard," Yuki said, her voice heavy with emotion. Her fingers lightly traced the contours of Yasufe's rugged face. She shyly looked into his eyes, searching for something.

It had been almost seven years since last she had seen Yasufe, the formidable warrior she had come to know in just a single night.

His once robust figure, though still imposing, bore the unmistakable signs of age and strife.

There was no doubt hers did too.

The relentless years of war and conflict had etched themselves on Yasufe's visage, where streaks of gray now mingled with his dark hair. Yet, Yuki found herself drawn to him with an undiminished intensity.

"Where have you been all these years?" she asked, her voice filled with joyous excitement.

"I have been serving as a warrior," Yasufe replied, his words carefully chosen to mask the full impact of his experiences. Yuki's smile beamed brightly as she marveled at his fluent Japanese, a stark contrast to his initial broken attempts during their first meeting.

"Your mastery of our language has improved greatly," Yuki remarked. "You must have carefully studied it. Back then, we could not speak; our only language was touch."

With her fingers still entwined in his, she gently wiped away the remaining tears from her cheeks, using the back of her hand.

A sudden tugging at her kimono caught her attention. Amara, her eyes bursting with curiosity, asked in her innocent voice, "Okāsan, Am I permitted to ask, who is this man?"

Clasping Yasufe's hand firmly, Yuki turned her eyes to her daughter, preparing to introduce her to the man who had left an indelible mark on her life.

"Amara, this is Yasufe," Yuki said softly, her voice trembling. "He is an old friend, someone very dear to me from many seasons past."

Yasufe bowed slightly to Amara, his eyes gentle and warm.

"It is an honor to meet you, young one."

With a touch of hesitancy, Yuki began to weave a simple tale for young Amara. "Long ago, Yasufe came to our land as a stranger. We became friends, and he left a lasting impression on my heart."

Amara, though young, was far from naive. She perceived a depth in her mother's emotions that the explanation did not fully capture.

Yet, she chose to hold her peace, instead suggesting that they return home and extend an invitation to her mother's friend to join them. Turning to Yasufe, Yuki's eyes were searching.

"Shall we do that?" she asked. "Do you come as a passing breeze, or will you stay longer than during our last encounter?" she asked with hope and uncertainty. "Will you join us, at least to eat?"

Yasufe held her gaze, his expression earnest. "I will remain for the night or a few days, Yuki," he promised. "Tomorrow, we shall share our stories and speak of what has passed."

As the midday sun bathed the land in its scorching glow, the trio journeyed toward the humble abode that had long since been serving as a home for Yuki and Amara. The path was lined with towering bamboo that whispered in the breeze, their rustling leaves creating a soothing symphony. The earthy scent of the forest floor filled the air, mingling with the faint aroma of wildflowers. But the beauty of the path was quickly ambushed by what Yasufe saw next.

Setting his eyes on the dwelling, Yasufe was overcome by a wave of disbelief. This rudimentary structure, little more than a repurposed livestock barn, seemed a disheartening shell barely adequate to shelter human life. The walls were weathered and worn, the roof patched with straw and reeds, and the air carried the faint, musty scent of aged wood and earth.

The domicile bore the markings of its former existence. Seasoned timber, worn down by the relentless passage of time, housed crevices and cracks like war wounds of their years of standing. Through these accidental peepholes, the insides of the house taunted the external world, offering tantalizing glimpses of the meager life within.

The makeshift roof was barely holding its own against the notorious rains that often came sweeping through the region.

The entryway was graced by two large doors hanging precariously, their once sturdy structure surrendering to age and neglect. The right door, its securing rope long since snapped, was grounded in the mud, while its counterpart was not far from sharing the same fate.

Yasufe, grappling with the grim reality, turned to Yuki with a shocked expression.

"Did they force you to live here?" he questioned, echoing the disquiet of his heart. "They exiled you here, in this place?"

Yuki looked away in a gesture that hinted, 'no.'

"We've made our home here for many a season," Yuki disclosed with a subtle undertone of perseverance. "The winters can be unforgiving, yet we've found ways to weather them. This place is all right. It is better than it appears at first glance."

Doubt overtook Yasufe's expression.

A silent pang of disbelief enveloped Yasufe while a whirlwind of emotions brewed within his stern façade. Yet, before he could articulate a response, the young Amara, unperturbed by his towering presence, grabbed his hand and guided him into their humble dwelling. "Here. Let me show you everything there is to see!"

A fleeting moment of surprise washed over Yuki; Amara was interacting with such ease with a man she had only just met! However, the sight soon brought a warm smile to her face.

Had she not done just the same thing? There was something special about Yasufe. Even now, she also trusted him implicitly.

"Would you please play Shogi with me?" Amara asked, her voice gentle. "My mother rarely has the time; when she does, I win."

"Certainly," responded Yasufe, obliging Amara's request. His willingness to keep Amara entertained brought an unspoken appreciation to Yuki's eyes. So much remained unsaid between them, so much history that needed revisiting, but for now, she was content with him building a bond with Amara.

As the duo dove into their board game, their laughter filling the quaint space, Yuki turned her attention to the hearth.

The soothing rhythms of preparing a simple meal of fish and rice served as a comforting background score to the newfound harmony unfolding within the home. Occasionally, Yuki looked at the two dotingly, lost in their own world of Shogi, hardly sparing her a glance.

As the day matured into late afternoon, the table bore witness to the remnants of their simple meal within the recesses of ceramic bowls. These leftovers soon became the object of interest for a group of tenacious flies. Emerging from her repeated defeats, Amara voiced her frustration. "Okāsan, I have lost six times! He is a very skilled player. How did you learn to play so well?"

Yasufe, his tone imbued with wisdom, replied, "Shogi, dear Amara, isn't merely a game. It's a mirror reflecting life's challenges and the art of defeating an adversary. It calls for a profound well of concentration, patience, and foresight. One must envision several moves ahead yet maintain the flexibility to alter one's strategy based on the opponent's tactics." Yasufe then winked at Amara, subtly pointing out her stubborn characteristics.

Caught in the playful whimsy of Yasufe's sarcasm, Amara decided she had had her fill of Shogi for the day. She yearned for the embrace of the outdoors, declaring her intent to play beneath the unblemished sky. Yasufe, too, longed for the same, seeking to drink in the fresh air.

More than that, though, the strategist within him saw this as an opportunity to examine Yuki's home and appraise its defenses.

Meanwhile, Yuki chose to remain within her house, intending to make it comfortable and inviting for the evening.

As she set about her tasks, Yasufe began his own.

He started by methodically appraising the entrances and exits, scanning the windows with a tactician's assessing eye, identifying potential weak spots, and formulating ways to reinforce them.

Next, he mapped the terrain, taking in the highs and lows of the surrounding land, his seasoned gaze seeking natural vantage points.

Then, he ventured toward the neighboring woodland.

Within its dense canopy, he studied the cover it offered and the concealment it could provide. It was a natural barricade, and he considered how to leverage it for protection.

Routes of approach were his next concern, identifying the clear lines and access points leading to the house.

From the seclusion of the woods, Yasufe watched the sun's arc across the sky, his eyes tracing the shadows as they danced around the tree trunks. His observant eye studied how both light and shadow played across the scene, mentally noting their respective patterns.

He didn't simply observe nature. The social landscape, too, held his interest. The ebb and flow of villagers, their paths, and routines were equally becoming etched into the canvas of his mind. Hours passed, and the light dwindled, but Yasuke, vigilant, missed nothing.

As the evening's soft twilight descended over the land, Yasufe found his way back to the humble dwelling. Upon entering, he found the interior warmly lit by candlelight, Amara already tucked away in the arms of sleep, and Yuki bustling about.

The table bore a simple yet welcoming meal: tsukemono, simmered fish, and freshly brewed green tea.

While Yasufe savored his meal, relishing the humble but heartwarming flavors, Yuki turned her attention to preparing the ofuro. The soothing scent of cedar filled the air as she poured hot water into the tub, steam rising to imbue the room with an ethereal quality as if spirits lingered in every crevice, waiting to dine.

Once Yasufe finished his meal, he began to disrobe, readying himself for the calming embrace of the prepared bath.

Placed centrally within the now cozy home, the tub offered a unique space for spiritual and physical cleansing.

As Yasufe stepped into the hot water, Yuki gently took a washcloth into her hands, ready to assist in scrubbing his body clean.

As Yuki moved her hands tenderly across Yasufe's skin, tracing the contours of his muscular figure, she unwittingly discovered a myriad of battle scars that marred his back. She flinched, recoiling.

"How did these come to be?" Concern weaved through her words. Yasufe remained in thoughtful silence, pondering if the time had come to unveil his history over the course of the last seven years.

Finally, he turned, his eyes meeting Yuki's with a depth that held her captive. "I did tell you of my role as a guardian," he began, his voice steady, "but what I left unsaid is that after our paths diverged, I found myself helping to lead an army of brave men under the command of Lord Oda Nobunaga."

Yuki's eyes widened; the name of Oda Nobunaga, the vicious but often celebrated unifier of Japan, was known to her.

Maintaining his stoic demeanor, Yasufe unveiled his truth.

There was a solid conviction in his voice.

"I was honored with the title of Samurai by the powerful Oda Nobunaga himself."

A profound silence consumed the room; the only sound was the consistent drip of water from the washcloth into the wooden tub as Yuki stilled to absorb his revelation, appearing pensive and anxious.

Yasufe pressed on, "I am no longer the man you once knew as Yasufe. My name is now Yasuke," he proclaimed, his voice a strong echo within the room's confines.

The sentiment reverberated in Yuki, who whispered, "Yasuke," almost in sync with him.

A flicker of surprise registered on Yasuke's face as he heard Yuki echo his new name. "You have heard these tales?"

"Yes," Yuki responded with a somber nod. "Of course. Everyone knows of the great unifier and his army, led by a remarkable black samurai. His strength and skill were unmatched in battle."

Her voice softened and she gazed at him just as fondly as all those years ago. "To think it was you, Yasuke, and that you survived those times ... it ... it brings warmth to my heart."

The truth was now laid bare; a swell of emotions had arisen within Yuki, joy at the reunion joined by a twinge of sorrow at the impending departure she feared. "If all you've shared is true, then I must prepare myself for your departure, yes? I assume it is your nature to seek new battles and conquests? That you cannot stay here for long. It will be just like last time."

With those final three words, she sighed.

Instead of a hasty reply, Yasuke allowed his contemplation to roam through the humble dwelling. He took in the roof with its gaping hole and the walls that bore visible scars of weathering and age. Finally, his eyes rested on young Amara, peacefully adrift in sleep, her delicate features dancing in the play of flickering candlelight.

A tender smile tugged at his lips as he gently cradled Yuki's face in his large, calloused hands.

"She is my child, is she not?" Yasuke asked suddenly, his voice barely a whisper.

Yuki's eyes softened, and she replied, her words laced with quiet certainty, "Isn't it quite apparent?"

Yasuke nodded, many emotions flickering in his eyes. "I had my suspicions after encountering your brother," he admitted. "But seeing Amara, it was beyond doubt."

Yuki took a deep breath, her stare turning introspective.

"Yasuke, when I discovered I was with child, I faced the harsh reality of raising her alone. The village, the people—they shunned us because Amara had been born of a foreigner with such dark skin.

"They whispered behind our backs, called her a curse, and treated us as outcasts. They refused us aid, barred us from their gatherings, and looked upon us with scorn. You cannot imagine ..."

She paused, her voice trembling with emotion.

"This morning, I struggled with how to broach this subject. I did not want to impose this responsibility on you without prior conversation, and more importantly, did not wish to reveal this to Amara without certainty of your intentions to stay. She deserves stability, not fleeting moments of connection, then an absence."

Yasuke's expression softened as he reached out to gently clasp her hand. "I understand, Yuki. I cannot change the past, but I am here now. I have choices. I can mold the future to be kinder to you both."

Yuki smiled, despite not knowing what any of his words meant.

Yuki resumed scrubbing his body, her eyes shimmering with unshed tears reflecting in the candlelight.

Yasuke released a deep, rumbling sigh and continued to speak. "Yuki. I have no intention of leaving. I will stand by your side while we raise and protect our daughter together if that's what you wish. As long as life stirs within me, you will face no disrespect again."

Before Yasuke could utter another word, Yuki leaned closer to him. Her eyes were filled with emotion, conveying a depth of feeling that words could not fully express.

"Yasuke," she began softly, her voice trembling. "Thank you for understanding."

She bowed her head slightly, a gesture of respect and gratitude. Yasuke, sensing the significance of the moment, lifted her hand to his lips and placed a tender kiss on it. This intimate yet respectful gesture spoke volumes of their bond and the journey they were about to undertake together in raising their child, Amara.

In that silent exchange, Yuki felt unparalleled reassurance and protection; they would face the challenges ahead as a united family.

CHAPTER THREE

In the Blood

(血の中に)

As the first light of dawn broke, it was accompanied by the incessant symphony of birdsong. Yuki stirred, a smile playing on her lips as she recalled Yasuke's pledge to stay. Opening her eyes, she found his place vacant. An undercurrent of anxiety momentarily unsettled her, but her eyes falling upon the tranquil figure of Amara, still in the embrace of sleep, calmed her restless heart.

Perhaps, she pondered, *Yasuke has felt an irresistible pull toward the familiar call of the battlefield. Perhaps it is not his choice whether he stays or goes.*

Regardless, she didn't allow these thoughts to linger, focusing instead on the daily tasks awaiting her. Together with Amara, she embarked on the routine cleaning of the house from the previous night's feast, scrubbing stained clothing against the washing board.

Later, they set about hanging the garments under the sun to dry, tugging at each piece to ease out the wrinkles while they were wet.

As they concluded, Amara asked, "Where is Yasufe?" Her question broke the silence and made Yuki pause. Considering the uncertainty of Yasuke's return, she was unsure how to answer.

Summoning her courage, Yuki began, "Amara, Yasufe's true name is Yasuke. When we first met, he was a bodyguard. But now, he has become a samurai. He is also your ..."

Before she could complete her sentence, the distant thundering of horse hooves and the clattering of a wagon diverted their attention.

Yuki's heart leaped as she hurriedly pulled aside the clothes hanging on the line. There, approaching their home, was Yasuke astride a horse, a wagon heaving with an assortment of supplies in tow: bundles of wood; hay; ropes; and other assorted necessities.

Relief washed over her, the sight of his return assuaging her fears and reigniting the strength of her joy from the night before.

Amara's exuberance seemed to dance around her too as she rushed to meet Yasuke, like any other small girl meeting her father's return— only in this case, she had no awareness of that fact.

The magnitude of her emotions seemed to burst her tiny frame.

Yuki, with the past pressing down on her shoulders and cautious optimism in her heart, took graceful strides toward them.

The air was thick with anticipation as Amara's voice cut through it.

"Where did you get this horse? And what are all these things for?" Her eyes were large with curiosity. "And where will we put them?"

It was a fair question, one which made Yuki giggle.

Indeed, they were hardly blessed with storage space.

With a steadiness in his voice that matched his stature, Yasuke answered, "I acquired the horse from a seller in the market. These materials are for fortifying and mending. Your mother's home deserves the care, and I may remain here a little longer to make sure."

Amara's joy was hard to contain as she tried to hide a smile.

"With you here, perhaps I can learn and become a master at Shogi," she said, her voice holding hope and a playful challenge.

Yasuke looked down at her, his eyes softening.

"In time, young one. First, we have a home to rebuild."

"May I help, Yasufe? I mean, Yas-u-ke?" Amara asked, struggling with his name. She looked up at him with wide eyes, filled with the enormity of the revelation. "Okāsan told me your true name."

Yasuke dismounted his horse and lowered himself to meet Amara's view. "What else did she tell you?" he asked gently, searching for understanding in her expression.

Amara, with the earnestness of a seven-year-old, murmured, "Nothing else, I think." Her eyes narrowed in thought, trying to remember every word her mother had shared.

As Yasuke's fingers tenderly traced the curve of her cheek, Yuki stepped near, her eyes clouded with emotion.

She was sensing the gravity of what Yasuke was about to reveal.

Breathing deeply, Yasuke looked into Amara's youthful eyes. "Amara," he began, his voice steady and solemn. "I also have another name you do not yet know."

"Another name? Who needs three names?" inquired Amara, eyeing him suspiciously, her eyes narrowed.

He smiled briefly. "Amara, my child. It falls upon me in solemn duty to reveal that I am, indeed, the one called 'father' in your life's journey. Know this as a truth that binds us beyond mere blood."

The world seemed to pause for a moment. Amara's eyes darted across to her mother for confirmation before returning to Yasuke.

She instinctively held her small arm beside Yasuke's, comparing their similar hues. A bright smile lit her face, and she said, "Oh, I thought so! You're the only one I've seen who looks like me. And okāsan, she was so happy when you came. Now, I know it is true!"

Yasuke and Yuki exchanged glances of astonishment and pride, marveling at the intuition and perceptiveness of this young soul.

For the following three months, the trio, bound by newfound bonds and revelations, committed themselves to refurbishing their home. Trips to Midoriya were frequent as they sought materials to fortify and beautify the formerly ramshackle tiny dwelling.

Yasuke's skilled hands meticulously sealed gaps that had once betrayed their privacy, leaving no avenues for prying eyes. The once fragile roof of the old barn underwent a transformation under his diligent care, readying itself to withstand the onslaught of relentless winter snows and the torrential rains of spring and summer.

The doors, once slouching defeatedly in the mud, were also resurrected. Yasuke masterfully integrated a system of ropes and pulleys, breathing new life into the main entrance.

However, his ambition continued beyond mere repairs. Pausing from his samurai training, Yasuke carved out a space, adding an annex to the home: a dojo, a sanctuary for discipline and learning.

With their home transformed, it now evidenced Yasuke's commitment, ensuring Yuki and young Amara had a haven in which to thrive. Noting a few lingering structural needs, Yasuke concluded that another journey for wood was imminent.

As he prepared to mount his horse, the sound of quick footsteps approached. It was Amara, her eyes gleaming with adventure.

"Please, may I join you on your expedition?" she asked, gazing up.

Yasuke's eyes flickered with hesitation, yet he eventually relented to Amara's eager wishes. Before Yasuke had become a permanent presence in Amara and Yuki's lives, Amara hadn't ventured to the heart of the growing Midoriya for a long while.

This was the very settlement that, due to an unyielding societal hierarchy, had once cast her and her mother to its fringes.

In a society that placed immense value on lineage and social class, Yuki's position was precarious. As a single woman with a daughter, conceived with a foreigner no less, she had borne the brunt of many harsh judgments and veiled whispers. Her so-called 'indiscretions' had painted her in colors of disdain in the eyes of many.

But with Yasuke by their side, the promise of protection lingered, brushing away past memories. As they rode, a gentle wind blew, playing with the rice fields, making them dance as if nature were generously orchestrating a ballet for their journey.

Yasuke, ever attentive, adjusted Amara's position on the saddle to ensure she had the best vantage point to appreciate the landscape.

They ventured beneath an avenue of wisteria trees, their cascading lavender blooms brushing softly against Amara's fingers as they passed, leaving traces of a gentle and heady scent.

The continuous hoofbeats echoed their progressing closeness.

With each step, Yasuke told Amara stories of distant lands, fierce battles, and tranquil beauty.

Each word painted a vivid picture in young Amara's mind. She imagined herself in his shoes, wandering through those foreign terrains and facing the world's wonders.

Approaching Midoriya, the rustic beauty of the scenery gradually gave way to an array of bustling life. Modern structures replaced ancient shrines, merchant stalls overflowed with goods, and the lively chatter of commerce filled the air. This transition from old to new captivated Amara, who clung wide-eyed to Yasuke's robe, attempting to take in every sight and sound.

There was a mosaic of the ever-changing world around her.

Yasuke guided the horse and wagon to a familiar merchant's stall, known for its quality wood. Dismounting with practiced ease, he gently assisted Amara down, her feet lightly touching the cobblestone path. As Yasuke haggled with the merchant, Amara was drawn to the vibrant life behind the wagon. The clamor of the market enveloped her: animated conversations; the clinking of sake cups; vendors hawking freshly caught fish; farmers boasting of bounteous harvests.

A protective hand rested on Amara's shoulder, bringing her attention back. "What's on your mind?" Yasuke inquired, glimpsing the wonder in her eyes.

"Oh, it is nothing really. I just … I wish we could visit this place more," Amara whispered, her voice filled with longing.

Yasuke's eyes darkened momentarily, his protective instincts surfacing. "These places can be unpredictable for a young girl like you, and especially for those who look different like us." He began gesturing toward the crowd. "See how they stare and whisper? We are different, Amara, and that makes them ever curious. It can make us feel uneasy, but our heritage is strong. Your mother's and mine.

"We are proud people, and we do not back down because of how we look." Unfazed, Amara's youthful spirit was still shining.

"I can stand up for myself," she proclaimed.

Yasuke's stern expression melted into a smile, admiring her courage. "Amara, you are my child, so I have no doubt of it."

Without another word, he led her back to the merchant.

Shortly after, the merchant's assistants busied themselves, heaving the purchased wood onto their waiting wagon.

Gently lifting Amara onto the saddle, Yasuke prepared to return to Yuki. The unmistakable hum of whispered conversations reached his ears. Though the chatter was distant, certain words caught his attention. It wasn't the native tongue of Japan but Portuguese, a language in which Yasuke had become fluent during his younger days, serving on fishing boats with Portuguese traders.

He discerned snatches of the conversation, the tone veering toward disrespect. Yasuke's focus sharpened, noticing the men's glazed eyes and sloppy postures, clearly inebriated from the many sake tokkuri flasks cluttering their tables.

Deciding it best to leave swiftly, he nudged his horse forward. But as they began to move, a man, unsteady on his feet, blocked their path, and soon, three others joined him, effectively hemming them in.

The leader, his voice slurred, sneered in Portuguese, "That's quite the steed for a kaffir such as yourself. Did you thieve it?"

Unruffled by the derogatory remark, Yasuke maintained his calm, attempting to steer clear and continue on their journey.

However, the intoxicated man boldly closed the distance between them, seizing the horse's bit in a foolish attempt to halt them.

"You think you can leave with this stolen horse?" the man slurred.

Yasuke's tone was icy as he retorted in fluent Portuguese, "For your well-being, step aside."

Surprised, the man questioned, "How does a kaffir like you speak my language?"

Though Amara could not decipher their exchange, she sensed the escalating tension, regarding the men with fierce defiance in her young eyes. She remained her father's ally, also unflinching.

Just as Yasuke motioned for the horse to advance, in a sudden, ill-considered move, one of the inebriates snatched a sake ceramic flask from a nearby table and hurled it toward them. With its shiny frame reflecting the sun's rays, the flask spiraled menacingly toward Amara.

Yet, in a display of unparalleled reflexes, Yasuke, as if he had trained all his life for this specific moment, deftly caught the projectile in midair, preventing harm to Amara.

The air was thick with tension, and words no longer held sway.

With the agility of a panther, Yasuke dismounted, his movements fluid and precise. As the first man lunged, aiming a fist at Yasuke's face, he effortlessly sidestepped, catching the man's wrist midair.

Yasuke channeled the momentum with a swift pivot, sending the attacker sprawling to the dusty ground in a mere heartbeat.

Another opponent lunged forth, fists flying in a frenzy.

But Yasuke's movements had become a dance, each step a masterful evasion. Every swing, every attempt was rendered futile against Yasuke's honed instincts that appeared effortless.

Adopting a jujutsu stance, he awaited his chance. When it came, he capitalized on his assailant's aggressive energy, redirecting it. He toppled this man too with minimal effort, leaving him disoriented.

By this time, whispers were spreading among the onlookers, their stares shifting to a third man advancing on Yasuke.

This man's eyes, which had held malice when hurling the flask at Amara, now held alcohol-fueled courage. He took a breath, steeling himself, before rushing at Yasuke.

With graceful agility, Yasuke skillfully ducked, again using the man's own forward momentum to his own advantage.

Grasping the adversary with a firm grip, Yasuke used his strength to launch him into the air. The attacker's shocked expression was frozen in the brief second he hung weightless before gravity took hold. But even before he could crash to the ground, Yasuke was there, pinning him, his dominance evident to all who watched.

But the confrontation was far from over.

The first adversary, now back on his feet, had found a weapon, the sturdy handle of a broom. Yasuke, feeling the wind shift, evaded the initial swing with a graceful sidestep.

From her perch atop the horse, Amara's eyes displayed wonder, her body subtly mimicking each of Yasuke's defensive maneuvers.

The assailant's second swing came in faster, desperation evident in its arc. But Yasuke was ready. With a quick motion, his hand closed around the handle, halting its trajectory. The stunned look in the attacker's eyes was all the opening Yasuke needed. He snatched the broom from the man's grasp and landed a decisive strike in one fluid motion. The attacker crumpled, knocked into unconsciousness.

The community, which moments ago had been buzzing with activity, had transformed into a silent amphitheater of stunned faces.

Yasuke, ever the stoic guardian, discarded the broom atop its former wielder, leaped onto his horse, and nodded to Amara as a silent confirmation indicating it was time to go.

With a nudge, they vanished into the woods.

The journey back to their home was painted in contrasting strokes of silence and enthusiasm. Yasuke, lost in his thoughts, let the rhythmic trotting of the horse blend with his introspections.

Beside him, Amara's eyes sparkled with both amazement and a touch of pride in this impressive man known as her father. She animatedly recounted the skirmish, her small hands mimicking the moves she had seen, emphasizing Yasuke's effortless takedowns.

Her physical excitement eventually transformed into a serious tone, capturing Yasuke's attention.

"Can you teach me?" she began hesitantly. "Not just how to defend myself, but to be like you, like a samurai?"

Yasuke turned and glanced at her, seeing not just the wide-eyed child but also the spark of a determined spirit within her.

Yasuke replied, carefully choosing his words, "To be a samurai is not merely about wielding a sword. It carries responsibilities and traditions bound by time. A young woman has a place in society that is different. But strength and honor are qualities you can embody."

Amara's eyes blazed with determination.

"I wish to be more than just fulfilling my place in society! Okāsan always said a woman should aspire as far as her dreams can take her."

Yasuke's eyes softened, memories of his time with Lord Oda Nobunaga surfacing. Nobunaga, a man who had defied conventions, valued innovation and boldness in battle. Training Amara, he realized, wouldn't be so distant from the principles he held dear.

"You have your mother's spirit," Yasuke replied, his voice gentle but firm. "To strive beyond the limits set upon you is noble. But the path of the warrior is fraught with challenges. Is this something you are willing to take on?"

Amara nodded, her mood unchanged.

"I understand. I am ready to be your best student."

Yet, he could not avoid thinking that their world was bound by stringent norms, especially for women. He pondered the risks of secretly training her and the potential consequences for both.

For now, he chose to guard his thoughts, not revealing to Amara the storm of contemplation raging within him.

The duo finally reached their home, the familiar thud of wagon wheels and horses' hooves echoing in the evening air.

Alerted by the sounds, Yuki darted outside, her face showing much concern. They had been away far longer than anticipated.

Her voice trembled as she spoke.

"Yasuke, you were gone for a long time. My heart was heavy with worry. You and our child, both away so long …"

The weighty silence that followed was interrupted only by the horses' restless movements.

Yasuke and Amara exchanged a meaningful glance, their eyes conveying unspoken words. Neither had prepared for this moment, and their hesitation spoke louder than any words. They had not considered how they would relay the day's events to Yuki.

After what felt like an eternity in silence, Yasuke finally spoke, his voice echoing the gravity of everything that had happened.

"We faced some trouble at the marketplace. Harsh words turned to violence when a man threw a tokkuri dangerously close to Amara."

Yuki's fingers instinctively clenched the fabric of her kimono, her eyes widening.

Yasuke, noting her distress, added, "I swore an oath to shield you both from harm. And today, that meant confronting those men and taking them down. Tomorrow may bring a fresh peril, perhaps in a month, an even greater challenge. We will be ready for it.

"The winds of change blow stronger now. But we shall stand firm and prepared when they gust upon our doorstep."

"We?" Yuki echoed, her voice quivering.

"Yes, both of you," Yasuke declared, his voice steady.

"Throughout our return journey home, I found myself reflecting deeply upon our circumstances. This world can be ruthless, more so for women. It's high time Amara learns the ways to protect herself, something she is keen to take on. And you, Yuki, must not remain defenseless either. Instructing Amara protects both of you."

"But you swore to be the one to shield us from all harm," Yuki protested, her tone blending confusion and desperation. It came across as a plea, as if she felt he would abandon them.

"I did," Yasuke affirmed, locking eyes with her. "And I shall remain true to that oath, guarding you with every ounce of my strength and breath. However, time is not eternal, and neither am I."

Standing closely by her mother's side, the spark in Amara's eyes was undeniable, revealing surprise and delight at Yasuke's words.

It was exactly the commitment she had asked for. Yet, she worked hard to restrain her excitement, fearing that any overt display might make Yasuke doubt her maturity and readiness for such training.

"So, when shall we begin?" Amara asked, her voice tinged with eagerness yet also with respect.

With a solemn demeanor, Yasuke answered, "When I deem you are prepared."

Sensing a test in his words, she gently inquired, "And when might that be?" She was stubborn and relentless for such a young one.

"Tomorrow, we will begin your mental conditioning. As for the physical training …" Yasuke paused, staring deeply into Amara's eyes, "your dedication and progress will decide that."

As the evening draped its shadowy veil across their modest dwelling, the three of them were wrapping up their evening meal. Amara stood up with the final morsels consumed, excusing herself to retire for the night, leaving Yasuke and Yuki in the dimly lit room.

With concern in her eyes, Yuki sought further understanding from Yasuke about his sudden decision to train Amara. She was anxious.

Yasuke, aware of the tumultuous state of Japan, felt the scale of his responsibility now more than ever. The fragmented nation was in a state of relentless upheaval, the warring provinces turning the landscape into an increasingly treacherous battleground.

Gently taking Yuki's hand in his, the dim candlelight projecting shadows on his stern features, Yasuke spoke with depth.

"Since the fall of Nobunaga, the land has been plagued by unending strife. These are difficult times, Yuki. You know that."

Yasuke paused, allowing the gravity of his words to settle before continuing, emphasizing each word.

"You and Amara, in your current state, are exceedingly vulnerable. This cruel world teems with predators waiting for a chance. You are weak, easy targets for the merciless souls roaming our lands. I have taken time to improve and strengthen the dwelling house for you both, ensuring no predators can gain easy access, unlike before. But now, it is necessary to do the same for you and Amara.

"What is the point in a sturdy roof and thick walls if your bodies and souls can be captured and taken advantage of? What will we do, keep you and Amara within these four walls forever?"

Yasuke's brutal honesty caused a heavy silence in the room, punctuated only by the soft crackling of the candle flame. Yuki's eyes, previously filled with doubt and anxiety, were now locked onto Yasuke, absorbing every word, every emotion coming from him.

"When I am no more," Yasuke's voice grew low, echoing his commitment, "it will be up to the two of you to stand guard over this home, over these lands that have cradled our family."

Yuki felt a knot in her throat, but she said nothing, letting Yasuke continue.

"I have faced countless adversaries in my lifetime, and under my guidance, many men became legends of their own," he declared. A hint of pride sneaked into his voice. "But Yuki, none have shown the fierce spirit of Amara. That same spirit which burns in my veins, courses through hers. She is our child, our legacy. It is in the blood!"

As he drew a deep breath, Yasuke's eyes gleamed. "She may not don the armor of a samurai or wield their title. But the essence of the Onna-Bugeisha, the female warriors of our great land, is what I see in her, without a doubt. And that essence, that spirit, I shall hone and nurture."

With each sentence, Yuki could visualize the turbulent future Yasuke was forewarning.

His gaze intensified.

"The element of surprise lies not only in open combat but also in the shadows of politics. Amara's skills, honed in secrecy, can be a decisive force in this era of betrayal, where alliances shift like the sands beneath our feet."

Sensing urgency, Yuki leaned in closer, hanging on to every word.

"Political adversaries expect moves based on tradition and custom," Yasuke continued. "But what they won't anticipate is the strength and strategy of a woman, especially one as fierce as Amara. Her presence, subtle yet powerful, could be a hidden advantage."

The room fell silent for a moment, interrupted only by the tapping of the wind against the home's wooden panels.

"With Japan in such turmoil," Yasuke added quietly, "trust will become a rare treasure. We must forge alliances with those who share a vision for a unified Japan, not just those seeking war and power. We must navigate these dangerous waters with wisdom, and Amara … Amara will be central to this change."

As Yasuke's words settled, Yuki spoke gently and respectfully, her face a mask of concern. "Yasuke, Amara is still very young. I worry that such training may be too much for her. And … I fear that, for her future, she might be used as a tool in the political games of men."

Yasuke sensed the depth of her concerns. "Yuki, I understand your worries. My intent is not to turn Amara into a pawn or an assassin. I see in her a spirit who can bring about change, not just for us, but for many who are voiceless. She will be a symbol of strength, not ever a tool of war."

Yuki's doubts dissolved in the warmth of Yasuke's conviction.

She stepped closer, wrapping her arms around him, sealing her understanding and trust with a heartfelt embrace.

CHAPTER FOUR

Let the Games Begin

(ゲームを始めよう)

As the cherry blossoms of the sixth week fell, marking the swift passage of time, Amara found herself growing increasingly restless. Yasuke had given his solemn word to Yuki and herself that he would mold her in the tradition of the Onna-Bugeisha.

Yet, the promise of mastering the blade seemed still so distant as no combat training had transpired. Instead, each sunrise saw the two of them deep in thought, maneuvering pieces on a Shogi board.

The strategic game had its merits, but to Amara's mounting irritation, victory still managed to elude her every time.

Yasuke, perceiving her frustration one morning, picked up a Shogi piece. "Amara, do you know why samurai often prefer a blade's cold precision over a cannon's thunderous power?"

Holding the piece up to the light, he added, "It's all about understanding the value of each move and each piece, just as it is in Shogi." Yasuke continued, "They all play an important part regardless of rank, similar to samurai in battle. "You will never beat me in Shogi, Amara, if you let impatience and anger rule your spirit. These emotions show in your play."

Amara's eyes, previously clouded with frustration, now smoldered with a stubborn fire. Her face gave away her introspection.

Yasuke recognized the change in her demeanor.

He would shift course.

"Perhaps," he began, "we should quit for the day, allow the teachings to seep in."

But Amara's spirit wasn't to be crushed so easily. She met Yasuke's eyes with fire in her eyes.

"No, otousan, teach me deeper into the strategy. By the week's end, I vow you shall face defeat. You must prepare yourself for it."

Yasuke's lips curled into a soft smile.

"The moment you can center your mind and defeat me on this board, we'll move to the dojo. But first, you must prove mastery over the battlefield of the mind."

Yasuke began by cracking his knuckles.

"You see, each time you make a move, you exercise strategy and foresight, much like a samurai anticipates his opponent's next move. It's a dance, a prediction of the future based on the present," Yasuke pondered, guiding the piece gently forward.

Amara leaned closer, her focus sharpening.

"And sometimes," Yasuke continued, "we sacrifice a pawn, not out of negligence, but for a greater gain, much like a samurai might sacrifice momentarily for a greater victory down the line."

She watched as he captured one of her pieces, turning it around to place it amongst his own. "Adaptability," he whispered. "In Shogi, a captured piece becomes a vital part of your army. On the battlefield, a warrior might find himself wielding a fallen enemy's weapon or using their strategies. Adapting is surviving."

She felt her frustration diminish, replaced by a budding understanding. Amara finally understood that the Shogi board was a strong mirror of warfare. Every piece, from the pawn to the rook, had value, much like every warrior, irrespective of his rank.

"When your pawn crosses the river and gets promoted," Yasuke said, showing her the move, "think of it as a young warrior proving his worth, rising in ranks, becoming more formidable."

Amara's eyes darted to the king, shielded by her pieces.

"And the king?" she asked.

"Ah, the king … Protecting the king is paramount, Amara," Yasuke emphasized, his stare hardening.

"Much like our sworn duty to protect our lord or daimyo with every breath." Thoughts of protecting Lord Oda Nobunaga started resurfacing in his mind as his words tapered off.

Over the following two days, the duo immersed themselves profoundly in the intricate strategies and nuanced tactics of Shogi.

The matches were long, testing Amara's mental fortitude, akin to a samurai's endurance during prolonged sieges. And with every game, she learned the value of etiquette and respect, bowing to Yasuke at the beginning and end, reflecting the samurai's code of honor.

Amara was enjoying a newfound respect for the game. Under Yasuke's new approach, the parallels between Shogi and the ways of the warrior were becoming clearer. Amara began to see that her training was not just in the swift strike of a blade but also lay concealed in the silent, calculated, and stealthy moves on the board.

The game was molding her, not just as a warrior but also as a strategist, embodying the very essence of the samurai.

The sun marked the midpoint of the fifth day since their last battle. Inside the humble abode, a fierce battle had begun raging, not of swords, but of intellect and strategy. The intensity of the Shogi match between Amara and Yasuke was palpable.

Each move paid back the hours of training and deep reflection, with both players fully engrossed in the duel.

Outside, Yuki made herself busy, preferring the serenity of nature to the electric tension inside. She knew that any intrusion might disrupt the balance of this critical match.

Now and then, a bead of sweat would roll down Amara's temple, a clear sign of the mental exertion and the pressure she felt, standing on the cusp of potentially besting Yasuke for the first time.

Yet, Yasuke, as if chiseled from stone, remained unyielding and poised. His expression mirrored that of a seasoned samurai, stoic in the face of challenge, revealing no hint of any storm raging within.

Back and forth they continued, a fierce contest of wits raging on the Shogi board. Each piece moved with careful deliberation, a silent battle of two equally determined minds.

Yasuke, sensing an opening in Amara's defenses, began capturing her rooks with quiet confidence. He believed the young prodigy's mental reserves must be depleting by now, a natural shortcoming of her tender age. But as he grew more audacious in his advances, Yasuke suddenly found himself trapped in a web of his own making.

Amara, with the wisdom and cunning that belied her mere seven years, had baited him into exposing his vulnerabilities.

Her bishops slid effortlessly across the board, slicing through his weakened lines. Her knights danced menacingly, applying relentless pressure from angles Yasuke hadn't anticipated. *Is it luck, or has Amara strategically placed me in this predicament?* he thought, enthralled.

Yasuke's usually composed face betrayed a hint of panic. With each passing move, his position grew more perilous.

Amara's strategy was clear: encircling him, closing in, move by move. And then, in a defining moment, the tremendous silence pressing upon the room was shattered by the glaring vulnerability of Yasuke's King Gyokushō, alone, defenseless, and under threat.

Amara raised her stare to meet Yasuke's, triumph on her small face. He, still stunned, retraced his moves in his mind.

Moments later, acceptance dawned upon him, and he began to applaud, the sound echoing throughout the room.

Amara, beaming with pride, gracefully rose and bowed.

"Do not stifle your joy, Amara," Yasuke proclaimed. "This victory is a tribute to your prowess and dedication. It is a moment to be cherished. You have proven yourself ready for what lies ahead."

"Arigatou!" she playfully shouted, her smile radiant and infectious.

She drew close to Yasuke, wrapping her arms around him and pressing her head to his sturdy chest. "Did I not say that I would defeat you soon?" she challenged. "It is due only to your lessons. You are a great teacher. I am prepared for every lesson," she whispered.

Yasuke, typically unruffled, found himself moved by the warmth of the moment. Gently embracing her, he said, "Your young heart indeed holds wisdom beyond its years; it will serve you well." He paused, his voice thick with emotion. "Celebrate this day and embrace your triumph." He gently nudged her toward the outdoors.

Amara, flushed with victory, let out a joyful squeal and dashed toward the doorway, her jubilant cries of, "I defeated him! I truly did!" reverberating through the air.

Yasuke stood there, a rare chuckle escaping his lips as her exuberant declarations gradually faded into the distance.

At the same time, Yuki stepped into their home, her arms loaded with fresh vegetables plucked from their garden.

Her eyes sparkled with curiosity.

"I can barely believe my own ears. Has she really bested you?"

Yasuke gave a nod, his voice soft with restrained pride.

"Yes, she managed to outplay me in Shogi."

Yuki raised an eyebrow, playful suspicion evident. "You let her win on purpose?"

Yasuke retorted, "No! I would never! She's not just my daughter but also my pupil. She must earn every accomplishment. Tomorrow marks the onset of her next challenging training phase."

Yuki, concern evident, interjected respectfully, "She is still so young. She has only seven winters behind her, Yasuke."

Yasuke replied, "She is extraordinary, Yuki. While I may lack the experience of raising many children, I recognize her exceptional maturity and intelligence. Trust me, she is ready for this."

In Yasuke's eyes, Amara's brilliance shone unmistakably. He recognized in her the same burning spark that had once ignited his youthful spirit. As a mere boy of five years old in his homeland, he had joined his elder brother in the hunt, swiftly becoming the most adept amongst in his village within a mere two months.

That same voracious hunger for excellence dwelled within Amara, and he felt an intrinsic call to harness and mold it. He was resolute in ensuring she would blaze her own path, just as he had.

The following day, the area was quiet, with only the distant chirping of birds to greet the new day. In the stillness, Amara rose, a new fire in her, ready to embark on her journey as a warrior.

Yasuke awaited her outside their home in a nearby field, his silhouette outlined by the emerging sunlight. His stance was poised with the serenity of a seasoned warrior. Each blade of grass seemed to hold its breath, acknowledging the dawn of a significant moment.

As Amara approached, her tiny feet padding softly against the earth, her silhouette merged with Yasuke's, symbolizing the merging of master and apprentice. The air was thick with anticipation.

Without a word, Yasuke handed her a bamboo bokken stave.

The weight felt foreign in her hands, yet there was an innate connection, a promise of power and discipline.

"I have learned that the path of the samurai or an Onna-Bugeisha is not just about wielding a weapon, Amara," Yasuke began. "It is about understanding oneself, harnessing inner strength, projecting it outwards. Today, we start with the basics, grounding you in movement and stance."

Amara nodded, accepting the burden of responsibility.

The morning pressed on, and the sun rose higher, casting a shimmering haze over the training ground. Birds and cicadas provided a pleasant ambiance, but they offered a mere backdrop to the dance unfolding between father and daughter.

Yasuke, sensing her determination, raised his bokken.

"Remember, Amara, in battle, it is not just about strength but also the rhythm, the precision, and speed. You will never defeat a male adversary if you're trying to match strength for strength. This must be a connection between mind, body, and blade. Every move should flow like water, not strike like thunder."

Amara absorbed his words, nodding slowly.

"Like the river that flows swiftly around the rocks, not trying to break them, but passing them," said Amara.

"Exactly," Yasuke acknowledged, his eyes shining in delight at her graceful analogy. He began a series of fluid movements, exemplifying what he had taught, and that of which she had spoken. It was like watching ink spread in water: seamless, graceful, with purpose.

Amara then tried to match his elegance, focusing less on force and more on rhythm and fluidity. They moved in unison, the bokkens creating a harmonious melody as they clashed, dodged, and twirled.

Hours seemed to drift by in mere moments, and with each passing minute, Amara's movements became sharper, more instinctual.

In the shadows of a fast-sinking sun, Yasuke, seeing the day's progress in Amara, deemed it fitting to conclude their session.

"The shadows grow long, and supper awaits," Yasuke proclaimed, his voice steady. "At the break of tomorrow's dawn, we will meet here. Day after day, we will persist. We shall also weave the endurance tasks with lessons we'll begin in the dojo."

Amara's eyes sparkled mischievously as she declared, "Who needs a dojo when I can strike with the swiftness and agility of a cat?"

As she spoke, she shaped her fingers to resemble the sharp claws of a feline playfully swiping the air.

Yasuke found himself charmed by the moment.

Setting aside his warrior's stance, he responded with an exaggerated recoil, playing into her fun. As the amber hues of twilight painted the sky for a brief spell, they basked in a simple, enchanted interlude, shedding the weight of their rigorous training.

Finally, with a tired shuffle, Yasuke and Amara stepped into their home, weariness evident in their posture.

A comforting sight greeted them, a supper spread beautifully laid out. Fresh white rice in the bowl, Amara's favorite fish delicately cooked, and freshly harvested vegetables from Yuki's garden were arranged alongside a pot of aromatic tea.

Amara, her hunger overtaking her fatigue, made a beeline to the wooden water basin, eager to cleanse herself before the meal.

Yuki's heart had been filled with unease all day, worrying about her daughter's ability to cope.

She watched as Amara scrubbed enthusiastically, relieved that her daughter was apparently okay, but she was still concerned.

"How did it go, my little blossom? Was it too difficult?" Yuki asked, her voice reflecting relief and concern.

Amara looked up, water droplets on her lashes making her eyes shine even brighter.

"It was enjoyable, okāsan! The time passed swiftly."

Yuki's gaze turned to Yasuke, accusation in her tone. "You allowed her to rest, did you not?"

Yasuke, raising his hands in a gesture of defense, replied, "She possesses more strength than you realize. I ensured her well-being. As you see, she is full of life. More animated than ever."

Amara chimed in, barely containing her excitement. "Tomorrow, we go to the dojo! I can hardly wait."

The corners of Yuki's lips slowly lifted, her concerns easing slightly. She bent down, planting a soft kiss on Amara's forehead. "Eat well, my child. Your enthusiasm brings warmth to my heart."

Witnessing the unconquerable spirit within her daughter, Yuki came to a profound realization. She could no longer confine Amara within the comforting cocoon of her maternal instincts. Yasuke's words echoed in her mind, reminding her of his broader vision for Amara, one that shattered the social norms for women of Japan.

The hunger and determination of which Yasuke often spoke were now undeniably apparent in Yuki's eyes. Seeing her daughter return, still radiant after a grueling day, she understood this was not merely a fleeting fascination for Amara, but a calling.

She could not, and would not, stand in its path.

CHAPTER FIVE

Growth and Conquest

(成長と征服)

Time, in its relentless march, had spanned seven swift years. Amara, once the child who used to find delight in life's simplest joys, had transformed. Now fourteen, she was radiating the energy and focus of a dedicated warrior, her infectious enthusiasm having matured.

Now, she exhibited a well-honed willpower.

Before the rooster signaled a new day, she was already on her feet, her figure retreating toward the snow-capped peaks looming in the distance. The chill did little to deter her; it seemed to invigorate her as she traversed the snowy forests with swift and graceful movements.

Gone were the days when she used to practice with the humble bamboo; now, her hand gripped a katana's cold, uncompromising steel. Its blade, polished to perfection, caught the winter sun, reflecting its brilliance, glinting toward the sky.

Under Yasuke's seasoned guidance, Amara's technique had only flourished, fusing age-old traditions with her innate flair, achieving artistry in every strike.

Yasuke rigorously instructed Amara in the art of kenjutsu, the noble path of the sword. Although Amara had not yet faced a living opponent with her blade, her skill was evident in the delicate dance of her katana slicing fruit in midair, each motion harmoniously combining precision and speed. It left Yasuke in quiet awe, realizing that Amara's prowess had eclipsed even his achievements at that age.

Even though she was just fourteen, it was indisputable that anyone brave or foolish enough to challenge her would likely face a swift, poetic end with barely time to think or realize what was happening.

Yet, change was not limited to Amara alone. Yuki, stirred by her daughter's fierce dedication, sought wisdom from Yasuke.

No longer content to remain on the sidelines and no doubt inspired by her daughter's efforts, she began her own journey, seeking to awaken the dormant warrior in herself.

Yuki's dedication to kyūjutsu—the revered art of archery—saw her arrows finding their mark impeccably, even at a staggering fifty yards' distance.

The tranquil evenings were no longer just a time of rest for Yuki; they became paramount to the family's dedication to martial arts.

The courtyard resonated with jujutsu's rhythmic footfalls and grunts as the sun dipped below the horizon.

Amid the physical training, Yasuke instilled in both Amara and Yuki the discipline to hone their minds as fiercely as their bodies.

He emphasized the importance of separating the heart's passions from the mind's clarity, knowing that a calm mind might prove to be their saving grace in combat. As the dusk draped its quietude over their home, they'd often sit together, embracing the practice of Zen.

They nurtured their emotional intelligence through meditation and mindfulness, fortifying their self-awareness and empathy.

Yasuke and Amara frequented the settlement's center, seeking wood to expand the dojo's space. On such sojourns, they would invariably cross paths with Yuki's estranged brother, Takeda. Though their encounters were silent, Yasuke often noticed Takeda's eyes lingering on Amara with curiosity and an inscrutable unease.

To Takeda, Amara was a distant memory, a niece last seen in her infancy. Now, nearing adolescence, her mixed heritage seemed to weigh on his consciousness. Yet, Amara's discipline was relentless.

She never allowed the shadows of prejudice to disturb her serenity, nor did she seek to confront her uncle about his distance. To her, Takeda was just another face among the many in Midoriya.

This bore witness to her unwavering discipline.

On one particularly vibrant day in Midoriya, amidst the lively marketplace exchanges, Amara's attention was drawn to a young girl, perhaps of her own age, pleading with the merchants.

Clad in tattered rags, and with the trials of hardship evident on her soiled face, this girl stood out from her peers. In a society in which girls her age were usually shadowed by domesticity, this lone wanderer's presence began to gnaw at Amara's conscience.

Though their paths crossed with each subsequent visit, Amara never approached her. Still, questions loomed in her mind, paying homage to a burgeoning empathy. Who was she?

Why had she been left to fend for herself?

Did she not have a family who loved her?

The enigma of the young girl would haunt Amara's thoughts, each journey into the center of the settlement deepening the mystery.

A week later, during the chilled embrace of an early morning, Yasuke and Amara were concluding the last movements of their rigorous training. Yasuke turned to Amara, his breath a visible mist.

"We must journey to the market once more," he said deliberately. "We need more wood for the dojo and a Tawara sack of rice for our meals."

Amara nodded, her thoughts consumed by the image of the mysterious girl from their previous visits.

Would she see the girl again today?

With a firm glint in her eye, she thought out loud, "Today, I shall speak to her." With her heart full of empathy, she tucked away a fresh kimono and a warm blanket, hoping to offer them to the girl.

As they entered the bustling settlement's center, the two split.

Yasuke, ever efficient in his task, headed to secure their supplies. Meanwhile, Amara, clutching the garments close, scanned the early gathering crowds, seeking out the familiar face of the young girl.

But her search proved fruitless.

Yasuke, having procured the necessary items, soon rejoined Amara, noting her evident disappointment. "Did you have any luck locating the person you're looking for?" he asked.

Amara sighed. "No luck at all. She might have returned to her origins. Well, as long as she is safe and has what she needs."

Yasuke turned and meticulously loaded their belongings onto the horse-drawn cart. He gestured to Amara, suggesting she mount the horse too. However, as she began to move, a distant commotion from a merchant's stall caught her ear. She handed Yasuke the items meant for the young girl as she felt drawn to the disturbance.

Navigating through the crowds, Amara's heart lurched, spotting the girl she sought. The youngster had been cornered by her intimidating uncle, Takeda, and two of his ferocious workers.

What is going on? Could she have stolen something? Amara wondered.

Drawing near, Takeda's sneering voice reached her.

"Be gone from my stall, beggar! You are scaring away potential customers. Go and bother someone else."

The rough men seemed set on manhandling the girl away, but Amara, fueled by righteousness, dashed forward. "Release her!" she cried. However, the men were unyielding.

"Shut up!" they called out to Amara. "Do you want the same?"

Takeda, with a malicious glint in his eye, confronted her.

Amara could feel the blood raging from him.

"Is this lowlife a friend of yours? I should have known as much." Without waiting for a reply, he bellowed, "You and your mother are a disgrace to this family and this community."

From his vantage point, Yasuke's silhouette sat tall on his horse, visibly taken aback by Takeda's audacious rebuke. It was well known that Takeda hadn't interacted with his niece in years, and to greet her with such disrespect was beyond belief. Yet, Amara remained calm, her rigorous mental conditioning evident.

With the gathering crowd and Yasuke deliberately not intervening, Amara realized this confrontation was hers to address.

Protectively, she motioned for the girl to follow her.

Yet, in her peripheral vision, she detected a man from Takeda's crew lunging at the girl, shoving her viciously to the dirt.

Outrageous laughter from the man ensued.

Rising to the occasion, Amara aided the fallen girl. Surprisingly, the second man decided to charge Amara, his eyes wild.

Her senses sharpened, instinctively detecting the oncoming assailant. With a swift, fluid motion, she grasped his wrist with one hand and reinforced her grip with the other.

Executing a flawless jujutsu joint-lock maneuver, Amara applied pressure to the back of his hand with her thumb, her fingers curling around his wrist. She twisted his arm against its natural rotation, a maneuver both artful and deadly. The man let out a shriek of agony as the sharp pain went shooting through his arm.

Amara's hips pivoted with precision, and she grounded him with a decisive leg sweep. The man crashed to the ground, his breath in ragged gasps, overpowered by Amara's swift and efficient technique.

In an overly aggressive manner, the first man charged her.

But Amara was again swift, a lethal empi-uchi strike landing squarely on his throat, rendering him motionless.

The crowd gasped, astonished to witness a young maiden of Amara's stature displaying such prowess.

Amara tightly clasped the girl's hand and made a beeline toward Yasuke, giving a look of utter disdain toward her uncle.

As Amara swiftly mounted their horse, Yasuke gestured for the girl to climb into the cart. The racket of whispered speculations from the settlement square trailed them.

Once they had distanced themselves sufficiently from the heart of the settlement, Yasuke guided the horse to a stop, allowing for a brief rest and an overdue conversation. Amara, curiosity burning in her eyes, asked, "Might I have the honor of knowing your name?"

With reverence in her voice, the girl replied, "I am called Chiyo. Your courage and skill earlier … they were beyond anything I've witnessed. Thank you for coming to my aid."

Amara, her expression softening, ventured, "I am Amara, and this is my chichi-ue, Yasuke-sama."

Chiyo offered a graceful bow. "It's a privilege to meet both of you. My heart holds deep gratitude for your intervention. But I should be on my way now."

"Stay a moment, Chiyo. Your presence has not gone unseen on several of our trips. Please, take these: a fresh set of clothes and a blanket." With concern, she added, "Why does someone like you, seemingly without the comfort of family or home, walk the streets?"

A cloud of sorrow settled upon Chiyo's face, and her hesitant words began to flow, painting a picture of her past.

"I hail from Sunpu, a prominent town just a day's journey by foot from this village. My father was a brave merchant, traveling across many provinces, selling and trading goods."

The chilling whisper of the wind, intertwining with the rustling leaves, seemed to amplify the desolation of Chiyo's tale.

Yasuke and Amara leaned in, captivated by her words' gravity.

"On his return from Mino and Owari, his demeanor had changed, revealing to my mother the news of an impending tax coming to

Suruga, one we could not bear. They shielded me from the finer details, but the cruel world named me an orphan by next daylight."

Tears trickled down Chiyo's face.

"Why must I bear this weight at merely fourteen?"

Her voice was a shaky whisper amid her tears.

Amara, reassuringly, laid a hand on Chiyo's quivering shoulder.

"Chiyo, you are not alone. Not anymore. We stand beside you."

Chiyo's figure straightened, brushing away the remnants of tears that stained her cheeks. Clasping the garments Amara had provided earlier, her voice was edged with a delicate gratitude. "Your help today, and these clothes, I will not forget. But I cannot become a burden on you. It's time I left."

Amara's voice surged loudly. "Wait!" Her loud plea pierced the quiet. "Our aid is yours should you seek it! We wish to offer it!"

Yet Chiyo, her silhouette growing fainter, quickened her steps, melding with the shadows of the deepening woods.

Amara, her eyes shimmering with sadness and curiosity, fixed her eyes onto Yasuke. "What do you think happened for her family to forsake their own blood?" she asked, her voice quivering.

Yasuke's features hardened, his jaw setting. "I may not know now, but be certain I'll uncover the truth," he declared.

After pausing briefly, he spoke again with authority. "However, the time has come for us to leave quickly. Ready yourself for tonight."

Amara's brow furrowed. "Ready myself for what?"

"Retribution," Yasuke said grimly. "Those men will come back with vengeance in their souls. A man's pride is fragile, and you shattered theirs today. Trust me, in their feebleness, they will muster strength from their humiliation."

Understanding the gravity of Yasuke's words, Amara swiftly mounted their horse. As they sped away, the cart rattling behind them, her thoughts were not on the impending threat but rather were consumed by Chiyo's haunting tale and its many concealed secrets.

After a few wandering thoughts, Amara shifted her attention back to Yasuke's words. A hint of fierceness was evident in her voice.

"Why would these men come after me? Did our earlier encounter teach them nothing? If they dare approach, they'll rue the day."

The intensity of her anger was profound, but Yasuke pondered if it sprang from the impending threat or her lingering worry for Chiyo.

"Amara, men blinded by their bruised pride often walk into the very traps they wish to avoid. Now is the time to master your emotions, not let them master you." He paused, allowing his words to resonate. "If you're not ready, I shall face them on your behalf. However, if you stand, stand with purpose." Most fathers would not allow someone of Amara's age to face a potential threat like this. However, his confidence in Amara once again was ironclad.

He took a breath before emphasizing, "Your training allows you to disarm without resorting to death. In defense of our home, our honor, and the defenseless, strike with purpose, never with rage. The path of the warrior isn't painted with mindless bloodshed."

Upon reaching their home, Amara swiftly transitioned from the elegance of her kimono into the practicality of a hakama, a garment more fitting for combat. Yasuke, meanwhile, briefed Yuki on the impending situation. In the past, Yuki might have voiced her apprehensions, urging Yasuke to protect their daughter.

But now, recognizing Amara's burgeoning skills, Yuki opted to aid her in preparing for the looming confrontation, all doubt set aside.

Joining Amara inside, Yuki helped her don the hakama, infusing each motion with maternal warmth. "These men," she whispered, securing a fold, "might be too faint-hearted even to appear tonight." Yet Amara, recalling Yasuke's insights, felt a tingling anticipation.

Earlier, as the sun had stood high, Amara had appreciated her straw hat for its shade. More than that, it provided a semblance of anonymity. Seeing its potential as a distinct advantage in the impending clash, she chose to retain it.

Emerging from their dwelling, Amara was the epitome of readiness, every fiber of her being primed for the face-off, her trusty katana glistening faintly in the dimming light.

Yasuke and Yuki, ever-watchful, discreetly positioned themselves. They were hidden from the assailants yet close enough to spring into action should the need arise.

As evening fell, an eerie stillness claimed the surroundings. Amara stood resolute, the chilling breeze brushing against her face unnoticed, her inner energy pulsating with an intensity permeating the space around. Yasuke could feel the girl's inner strength, a palpable aura resonating through the stillness.

He glanced at Yuki, his voice deep and firm.

"Amara's spirit is strong; she could stand against a legion of men if they dared challenge her tonight."

With pride and anxiety, Yuki whispered in agreement, "Her energy is undeniable. I feel its force and no longer worry like I used to."

Suddenly, the arrival of the two men was signaled by the rustling of leaves from the shrouded tree line. Their silhouettes materialized from the gloom, an air of malevolence surrounding them.

Amara stood firm, her gaze steadfast, and her eyes showing not a hint of fear; her training with Yasuke had been relentless, honing her reflexes and sharpening her instincts. She felt more than ready.

She had sparred with the seasoned warrior on many occasions, learning to read movements and anticipate attacks. Drawing a breath to announce herself, she addressed the men with an authority beyond her age. "You should not have come here. What honor is there in seeking revenge against a young girl of fourteen years?"

The men hesitated momentarily, taken aback by Amara's poise and stern demeanor. Their previous altercation had taught them not to underestimate her, yet their bruised egos had been unable to resist this confrontation. Then, the voice of one of the men wavered, betraying his unease. "Earlier, luck may have favored you, young girl. But as night falls, you'll learn a harsh lesson. You'll soon see."

With these words, the second man drew forth his weapon, the light gleaming off the blade of a Yari spear.

With this in hand, he cautiously approached Amara.

Her voice, steady, warned, "There's still a chance to turn back."

But their pride and intentions clear, they continued their advance.

Resigned to the confrontation, Amara deftly aligned herself, her blade held aloft in the jōdan-no-kamae high guard stance.

A fleeting moment of doubt passed between the two men, their eyes meeting hesitantly.

With the spear raised high, ready for an attack, the man was wholly unprepared for Amara's swift precision. Like a gust of wind, she slid into position, slicing the spear's blade even before it began its descent. In the very next moment, and with a fluid motion, she positioned herself behind the men, her blade drawn close to the neck of the one grasping the spear.

The chilling sensation of cold steel met his skin, and a thin line of blood dripped down.

His breath grew ragged already, heart pounding fiercely.

Yield," Amara commanded, her voice a low, dangerous whisper. "Do you see now how easily your life hangs by a thread due to your misplaced arrogance?"

Not to be outdone and having a marginally better combat acumen, the other man snatched the splintered spear from his companion and launched an attack of his own, fierceness on his face.

With unparalleled agility, Amara ducked, severing the remainder of his weapon. Before he could gauge her next move, her sharp blade was pressed against his throat.

Sensing Amara's might, the first man began to inch away, his confidence shattered. Yet, the man beneath her blade's edge spat toward her, signaling his bitter acceptance of defeat.

"Look … look at you. You animal," said the man, gasping for air. "A foreigner like you shouldn't even be here."

"I was born on this soil; it is as much mine as yours. And unlike you, I can stand my ground and defend it," Amara retorted.

Just as Amara began to lower her weapon, sensing the confrontation's end, he shifted his weight and surged forward, attempting a surprise assault.

Amara sensed it and sidestepped gracefully as if it was nothing, letting him tumble past under his own momentum.

Rising quickly, she brought her katana upward, descending rapidly, halting just a hair's breadth from the man's jawline.

A tense, electric silence enveloped them as their eyes locked once again, each assessing the other.

"You will leave this place," Amara stated, her voice commanding.

As the man nodded slowly, seemingly in acceptance, his hand subtly reached into his kimono.

With a sudden flick of his wrist, he revealed a hidden blade and lunged at Amara in a last desperate attempt. Instinctively, she reacted, her katana slicing through the man's throat with lethal precision, and he crumpled to the ground, lifeless.

The world around Amara seemed to blur. She stood over the fallen body, her katana dripping with the man's blood. A numbness spread through her, her mind struggling to process the reality of having taken a life. The oppressiveness of the act felt like a sack of rice pressing heavily on her chest, her breathing shallow and rapid.

Yasuke, witnessing the turn of events, stepped forward, his expression holding both concern and sorrow. "Amara," he called softly, placing a hand on her shoulder.

"You did what was necessary. This was no frivolous act; had you not done it, you would have failed and become prey."

Amara's water-filled eyes were wide and unfocused as she looked down at the bloodied blade in her hand. Her voice was barely a whisper, trembling with shock. "I … I killed him."

"Yes," Yasuke acknowledged gently, "and it may not be the last time you face such a situation. But remember, you acted to protect yourself and those you love. It is a burden we must carry as warriors. Most importantly, you didn't kill out of revenge or pride."

Amara nodded slowly, the reality of her actions setting in.

Her emotions were a tumultuous storm, a profound numbness mingled with a growing sense of unease and the beginnings of guilt. Yet, she also felt a strange, unsettling sense of power, a flicker of something unhinged within her.

Yasuke's grip on her shoulder tightened, grounding her. He felt it fitting to downplay what had just happened to keep Amara's emotions in check. "You are strong, Amara. Stronger than you know. Do not let this moment define you. Let it be a lesson, a solitary step on your path to becoming the warrior you are meant to be."

With a deep breath, Amara sheathed her katana, her hands still trembling. "I understand, otousan," she said, her voice steadier now. "I will learn from this."

As the last man retreated into the night, Yasuke and Yuki watched Amara closely, their expressions displaying worry.

As they began their homeward journey, the subtle crack of a twig caused a fresh ripple of tension.

On high alert, Amara instinctively flung her sword toward the sound, only for it to embed itself into a tree trunk. A shadowed figure hesitantly stepped into focus, revealing none other than Chiyo.

She had observed the entire skirmish from her concealed hiding spot, having followed Amara and Yasuke since their last encounter.

With the sound of leaves crunching underfoot, Amara rushed toward Chiyo and reached her in mere moments.

She clasped Chiyo's hand, immediately apologizing for almost hitting her with her sword. Amara's heart was still racing from the adrenaline rush of the altercation.

However, Chiyo's eyes held not fear but admiration.

"I … I apologize for following, but your earlier kindness moved me, and I couldn't resist learning more about you," Chiyo said with caution. "Again, I am sorry. But I see dedication and discipline in your movements, Amara. I've never seen a woman take a man's life. It was intense. I wouldn't know how to cope with it."

Amara's eyes darkened momentarily, her actions settling, pressing harder on her now she was reminded of it.

"It will not be easy," she admitted quietly. "However, I have been trained to protect myself and those I care about, even if it means making difficult choices." She paused, her stare distant. "I do not know how I feel yet, Chiyo … It is as though my heart is numb. The reality of what I have done has not fully struck me."

Chiyo nodded, her voice reassuring. "Your actions were in self-defense, Amara. You did what you had to do. But it is normal to feel this way. You are strong, but also human."

Amara offered a small, grateful smile, appreciating Chiyo's empathy. "Thank you Chiyo! Come, meet my okāsan and otousan."

Chiyo bowed respectfully to Yuki and Yasuke.

Yasuke stepped forward, his voice calm yet firm. "The hour grows late, and we must seek shelter. Chiyo, you will be our guest tonight.

At dawn, you and I shall depart for Sunpu to reunite you with your kin. You three head back; I will remain here to address this matter."

Chiyo bowed again with gratitude and understanding.

The three of them began their walk toward the family home.

Amara glanced back briefly, watching Yasuke's massive silhouette as he hefted the man's body over his shoulder. Anxiety formed a tight knot in her throat. She then turned her gaze back to Yuki and Chiyo walking away. But it wasn't until she watched Yasuke again that Amara swallowed the nervous lump, accepting what she had to do: bury this night deep in the tombs of her mind.

She hurried to catch up, the promise of warmth and comfort guiding her steps through the deepening night.

As the first dawn light streamed through the window, Amara awoke, body and spirit refreshed despite the previous evening's ordeals. Yet, as she stirred, Yasuke and Chiyo were nowhere to be seen.

Sensing her daughter's confusion, Yuki explained, "Yasuke sought to reach Sunpu and return by sunset."

Yuki gently suggested Amara rest further, even as she busied herself, preparing a simple morning repast.

But Amara, ever faithful to the disciplined path of a warrior, felt the day beckoning her to resume her studies and hone her skills, just as she did every morning. Watching her, Yuki was struck by a profound realization; the fiery passion that had ignited Amara's spirit as a young child was as intense and firm as ever.

Yuki felt inspired by her daughter's dedication, joining Amara in her training. The two women, bound by blood and spirit, delved deep into their respective martial arts. With swift motions and an eagle's eye, Yuki masterfully demonstrated her skills in mobile archery, using trees as cover and consistently hitting her marks.

Meanwhile, Amara positioned herself atop a nearby hill, the rising sun creating an ethereal glow around her. Her sword danced in fluid arcs, slicing through the crisp morning air. Yet, beneath her poised exterior, her mind was still grappling with the previous night's events.

The faces of the men haunted her, and she reflected on whether she should have ended both men once and for all. Or how could she have been better? Her internal battle raged on with every thrust and parry, mirrored in her powerful yet graceful swordplay.

As her blade cut through the air, Amara's thoughts turned to Yasuke and Chiyo. Would Yasuke uncover the truth behind Chiyo's parents forsaking her? Had their journey been fraught with challenges? Amara maintained her disciplined rhythm despite the constant questions her mind persisted in throwing at her.

As the hours passed, Amara and Yuki reconvened in their tranquil courtyard for a short but spirited sparring session. Amidst their dance of blades, Amara's introspective demeanor was evident. "I wish Chiyo had remained longer. She felt … akin to a kindred spirit, someone who truly comprehends my essence."

Reading the longing in her daughter's eyes, Yuki said, "Paths that once crossed may cross again. Destiny has its own designs."

She was thinking of the fate that had first brought Yasuke her way, and how they had met again, so many years later.

Amara, however, seemed less convinced.

"The distance between us feels impossible."

Yuki noticed her daughter's distracted state and suggested they end their training. Together, they went inside to prepare for supper, eagerly awaiting Yasuke's return.

As the sun set, the sky daubed with amber and crimson hues, the sound of a galloping horse grew closer with each thunderous beat.

Amara and Yuki, recognizing the sound, readied themselves to greet their homecoming Yasuke.

The two approached him as Yasuke tethered his horse to its post. Soon enough, the towering silhouette of Yasuke approached them, his eyes betraying a smile beneath an otherwise serious demeanor.

However, just beyond his intimidating frame, a smaller shadow emerged. "Chiyo?" Amara bellowed with astonishment and delight.

She darted forward, her steps quickening. "Why have you returned? I mean I am glad but what has happened?"

As Chiyo opened her mouth to reply, Yasuke's stern command to enter the house halted her words.

Swiftly, Yuki set before them bowls of steaming udon and fragrant tea. The ambiance within the room grew thick with tension.

The four of them sat in solemn silence, the only sound being the subtle slurping of noodles and tea.

Yasuke, having finished, placed his empty cup on the wooden table, its sound echoing the magnitude of his forthcoming revelation.

He locked eyes with Amara and Yuki, his voice gravely serious as he began, "In Sunpu, under Chiyo's guidance, we reached her home, only to be met with visible hostility from her kin."

He recounted how Chiyo's father, Yasuo Kobayashi, after much persuasion, opened up about the unfolding chaos in their region.

"Feudal struggles are not uncommon, but the extent of the tyranny of one clan was never apparent to me until now," Yasuke murmured. "A warlord named Hideaki, and his son Yoshinori had taken Owari and Mino under their control and built an army impressive enough to challenge even the shogunate."

As Yasuke continued, his voice dropped to an even graver note. "Hideaki imposes ruthless taxes, and the so-called 'daughter levy' is most distressing. Families with unwed daughters of marriageable age face exorbitant taxes and failure to pay; in such a case, their daughters are taken. Many became servants, some even worse, condemned to serve the whims of Hideaki's heinous warriors."

A shadow of anger crossed Yasuke's face, his usual calm demeanor disrupted by this seething overtone.

"The Kobayashis, incapable of bearing this price, tried marrying Chiyo to her cousin in their desperation. Unable to bear the weight of their own choices, they renounced their ties to her."

The revelations dampened the ambiance within the room.

Amara, overwhelmed and disgusted, instinctively reached for Chiyo's hand for support, their fingers interlocking in a tight grip.

"Though I chose a life of peace …" Yasuke's tone shifted, reflecting a hardened commitment. "… I never let my guard down. My days of meditation, reflections on past battles, and consistent training were not just rituals. They were preparations."

Yuki quickly responded, "What's our next move?"

Yasuke rose slowly, his voice carrying resolution.

"We brace ourselves for the storm that's bound to hit Suruga. War is on the horizon."

Without another word, he moved with purpose toward the door.

As he reached the nearby woods, the first rain droplets fell.

His fingers dug into the earth, clods of cool mud clinging to his hands. The sudden intensity of the rain didn't deter him.

Following in quick pursuit, Yuki gestured for the girls to keep pace. As they navigated through the woods, rain now pouring, they spotted Yasuke's imposing figure. His hands, stained with mud, were finishing a task that had been buried and forgotten.

Raising his back to them, Yasuke revealed his legendary sword, Kurokaze, the Black Wind. As he turned, the blade glinted, the raindrops sliding off its dark surface. His voice, filled with an unmatched grit, echoed through the rain-soaked trees.

"I had hoped Kurokaze's time was past, a relic of old battles. Such hope was naive." His eyes locked onto theirs, each word dripping with weight. "No matter the time it takes, whether months, years, or decades, we shall stand and protect our home."

CHAPTER SIX

Resistance

(抵抗)

In the span of seven tumultuous years, as Amara blossomed into her own, a relentless struggle for territorial dominance raged in the background. War drums echoed relentlessly across the provinces as Lord Hideaki, alongside his zealous son Yoshinori, led the fierce seven-year tug-of-war. Their intent was to now grasp control over the strategic lands of Mikawa and Totomi.

Besieged and pressured, Mikawa's indomitable spirit held firm, resisting every attempt at complete subjugation.

Beyond the eyes of the realm, a political chess game of the highest order was unfolding. The emperor, luxuriating in Hideaki's lavish tributes, remained blissfully unaware of the intricate web being spun. In his astute wisdom, Shogun Tokugawa Ieyasu silently funneled resources into Mikawa, strategically bolstering its defenses.

While the chess pieces moved covertly in the background, the balance of power still started to tip in Lord Hideaki's favor.

Yoshinori stood at the vanguard of this fray, commanding an impressive army of three thousand men under his father's banner.

Though their numbers paled in comparison to the forces of the Tokugawa Shogunate, the Hideaki bushi held several aces up their sleeve, including their mastery of modern weaponry, a linchpin in their growing dominion.

Also, during this time, Yoshinori's strategic brilliance became unmistakably clear.

In the unyielding chess game of warfare, he was several moves ahead. With an innate knack for warfare tactics, his approach on the battlefield seemed unparalleled in its innovation and execution.

Drawing from a network of trusted informants, Yoshinori gained invaluable insights into enemy formations and plans. But his unconventional methods struck fear into the hearts of Mikawa and Totomi defenders. Via a shadowy alliance with ninja clans, he orchestrated a series of covert operations, targeting the enemy's lifelines. Supplies were sabotaged, food stocks were reduced to ashes, and arsenals were captured or destroyed.

His audacity knew no bounds; he even resorted to poisoning water sources, sending ripples of panic and uncertainty throughout the provinces. Despite his best efforts, the strategies he employed were not effective enough to help them turn the tide of the seven-year conflict in their favor.

On a gusty dawn, Yoshinori found himself perched on a cliff, his gaze scanning the scarred landscape of Mikawa below. The aftermath of the siege lay bare; the earth lay stained with the blood of countless warriors, their lifeless forms a testimony to the brutal clash.

Such sights might have shaken any man to the core, but for Yoshinori, they served only to ignite his fiery spirit.

His eyes soon caught a lone figure amidst the carnage, an older man with ragged attire scavenging through the pockets of the departed. A fleeting envy gripped Yoshinori, not for the man's status or impoverished clothing but for the ease with which he claimed the spoils of battle. The thought tormented him, that of the luxury of marching into Mikawa after all battles had been fought, with nothing left to do but claim the reins of control.

How nice it must be, he thought.

Then, the steady sound of armor and the commanding cadence of boots were heard approaching in the distance, but nothing could break Yoshinori's trance-like focus on the scene of carnage before him. That was until his father's familiar, firm hand rested on his shoulder. They shared a moment, taking in the battlefield's grim scene, cloaks billowing in the increasing gusts.

"Quite the sight, isn't it?" Hideaki's voice broke the silence, somber pride underlying his words.

"It's a brutal reminder," replied Yoshinori, his voice strained. "It reminds me that every drop of blood spilled must have a purpose, that our path must lead to victory. Otherwise, the sacrifices made will have been in vain. This panorama has haunted my mornings for a month now, reminding me of our purpose."

With fire in his eyes, Hideaki clenched his fist and thrust it close to Yoshinori's face, emphasizing each word. "Then harness this sentiment! With such fortitude, Japan will be under our power before age steals my strength and the inevitable shadows claim me."

The wind rustled through their armor, a momentary pause ensuing before Yoshinori decided to speak.

"Mikawa has proven more challenging than I ever foresaw," he mused, begrudging admiration in his voice.

Hideaki looked out into the distance, but his words carried weight. "A little sparrow whispered to me of Shogun Tokugawa's hand in fortifying Mikawa's defenses. Our tributes to the emperor seem to wane in significance these days." Pausing momentarily, Hideaki's voice turned graver, "Meanwhile, the shogunate's audacity grows. They stand on the precipice of overshadowing the emperor, reducing him to a mere ceremonial figurehead."

Yoshinori responded sharply. "Then we must act swiftly. Our strategy for Mikawa and Totomi will be redefined," he pledged.

"Once Mikawa and Totomi bend to our will, we set course for Shinano," Hideaki said, his voice echoing authority. "Its plains, ripe with rice fields, and its pastures, teeming with livestock, await us. A land of farmers and merchants who wouldn't pick up a sword against us if we paid them. It will be an easy conquest. To add, I have a history with the so-called Lord in that region."

Hideaki's face bore a sinister expression of satisfaction as he began to leave.

"Come, Yoshi!" Hideaki beckoned. "The sun still climbs in the sky, and there are strategies I wish to share with our bushi."

"In a moment, my lord," Yoshinori replied. Once assured of his solitude, he seized the chance for reflection.

Grasping the edge of his flowing cloak, he neatly folded it beneath him as he settled cross-legged on the ground, hands resting on the cool, dew-kissed grass, drawing in the raw energy of the war-ravaged land around him. He proceeded to meditate.

For Yoshinori, meditation was no mere practice; it was a doctrine. The embodiment of discipline, he reserved time daily to immerse himself in the meditative trance, meticulously crafting and revisiting his strategies. He believed fervently in the power of visualization; if he could clearly see an outcome in his mind's eye, then it was within grasp. The sweeping successes of the past seven years demonstrated the potency of these daily introspections. With this poignant backdrop, he now sought to contemplate further the tactics that would inevitably tilt the war's balance into their control.

As Yoshinori immersed himself in meditation, revelations about Shogun Tokugawa's backing of Mikawa's defenses crystallized in his mind. Recognizing the shogunate's thinly stretched forces, grappling with feudal skirmishes across several provinces, he perceived their inability to support Mikawa and Totomi further.

However, mere tactics of poisoning the water and disrupting food chains would no longer suffice.

He needed to employ a strategy that would catch them off guard.

A deceptive assault took form in his mind, a ruse he believed would be potent enough to entrap the shogun.

He envisioned drawing a substantial portion of his troops, about a third of his formidable army, toward Totomi, signaling it as the new primary point of contention. The hope was that this maneuver would compel the Shogun Tokugawa to reposition and allocate more significant resources to Totomi's defenses, thereby thinning out Mikawa's. Amid this deception, Yoshinori was plotting to swiftly deploy a battalion equipped with their vast collection of modern weaponry to establish dominance over Mikawa.

Gently rising from his meditative state, a newfound clarity coursing through him, Yoshinori descended the cliff to the war tent where the seasoned commanders of the bushi gathered, hanging on to Lord Hideaki's every word.

From a distance, Yoshinori could perceive the tension in the tent; the unmistakable sheen of sweat on the foreheads of the bushi commanders demonstrated the gravity of the discussions within.

"Yoshi," Hideaki motioned as he paused, allowing his son to join the inner circle. "We've been pondering tactics to pierce through these years of dogged resistance."

Yoshinori's heart raced with anticipation, the topic he wanted to discuss unfolding before him. The air in the tent was charged with excitement as he leaned in, eager to engage in the conversation.

Still, he remained composed, settling among them, keen to absorb the ongoing discourse and contribute his recently formed strategy.

Lord Hideaki's piercing gaze locked onto Yoshinori. He stroked his goatee contemplatively, his voice firm and magnetic. "As I mentioned, I was sharing with our esteemed bushi that our strategy needs recalibration. I promised them you'd be here to grace us with your tactical prowess to enhance our path to certain triumph."

The war prep hustle and clamor outside the tent contrasted starkly with the electric silence within; expectant eyes turned to Yoshinori.

Yoshinori replied respectfully, "I would be honored to hear your wisdom first, my Lord."

Yoshinori was adeptly aware of how to navigate his father's intricate web of cunning and overbearing pride. Hideaki, driven by a subconscious unease toward other dominant men, was notorious for attempting to bait and overshadow his son. Faced with such challenges, Yoshinori's tenacity was constantly tested.

He became skilled in sidestepping these confrontations, even as he grappled with his own deep-seated desire to assert his significance.

Lord Hideaki probed again, offering Yoshinori the chance to present his strategy to those gathered. Yet, Yoshinori, ever respectful of the subtle dynamics at play, firmly but politely demurred.

Hideaki's eyes sparkled with mischief and approval.

"Very well," he began. "I want to enlighten you with a tale from my younger days, one of the Battle of Okehazama, where the now-departed Lord Nobunaga, though never my ally, achieved the unimaginable. Commanding a modest force of two thousand to three thousand valiant souls, he dealt a crushing blow to the mighty Imagawa Yoshimoto and his staggering army of thirty-five thousand. A situation mirroring our own."

For some of the bushi, this tale was a revelation, their eyes widening in awe. Others nodded in fervent agreement, reinvigorated by the legendary feat that scarcely seemed possible.

Hideaki's voice rose, filled with conviction and enthusiasm. "We are our only obstacle!" he roared, his fist thundering against the table, inspiring an undeniable resolve in every man present.

Hideaki then surveyed the tent with intense eyes.

"We'll adopt Nobunaga's tactics, drawing from the past for inspiration. The heavens will be our ally. With each torrential rain, we shall launch our surprise assaults, catching them unawares. Yoshi!" Hideaki's voice boomed, ensuring all eyes were on his son. "Your men must be ever vigilant, ready to strike at a moment's notice."

Yoshinori met his father's stare with a solemn nod, acknowledging the command's seriousness. Internally, however, he couldn't help but ponder. While his father's strategy held merit, they would need something more exceptional to triumph in this long-fought battle.

Just as Yoshinori was about to voice the strategies he'd conceived on the cliff, Hideaki's imposing voice once again filled the tent.

"Additionally, I suggest we unleash rapid assaults under the cloak of night," Lord Hideaki continued fervently. "Our foes must never know rest. We shall sleep in shifts during the daylight, only to descend upon them with a storm's ferocity as darkness falls."

The tent resonated with the clapping and affirmative murmurs of the bushi, their faith evident in Lord Hideaki's tactics.

A pang of anxiety gnawed at Yoshinori; he feared his insights might stay unheard. While acknowledging his father's tactical prowess as the army's commander, Yoshinori felt an innate responsibility to infuse his own strategies, believing them pivotal for victory.

Absorbing the admiration around him, Hideaki looked supremely confident, almost as if the spoils of war were already theirs.

Recognizing the pressing need to make his voice count before his father concluded the talks, Yoshinori rose to speak.

"Your strategy is masterfully crafted, my Lord," Yoshinori began, a genuine admiration for his father's intellect evident in his tone.

Hideaki smirked. "Ah, Yoshi. Are you ready to eclipse your father with your ingenious tactics?" The playful mockery in his voice thinly veiled his true intent to challenge and provoke.

Yoshinori responded with both grace and confidence. "Far from it, my Lord. I merely wish to intertwine my insights with your already flawless blueprint." Pausing for a breath, he continued, "Building upon your night and rain tactics, might I suggest a diversion?

"We can relocate a third of our forces to Totomi. Such a bold move would mislead the shogun into thinking we've forsaken Mikawa entirely. And when he redirects his forces from Mikawa to Totomi in response, the veil of the night becomes our ally.

"We strike Mikawa with all the might of the shadows, reclaiming it in mere weeks, if not days. Once Mikawa is firmly within our grasp, we can then pivot, storming into Totomi with renewed vigor."

Hideaki's eyes sharpened, intrigued by Yoshinori's layered strategy.

As the war council concluded, father and son emerged from the tent, stepping into the cool embrace of the dawn.

The camp was now stirring to life even more.

The distinctive ring of whetstones sharpening blades blended with the low murmurs of soldiers preparing their muskets.

Amid this backdrop of disciplined chaos, Lord Hideaki turned contemplatively to his son, appreciating the potency of the strategy they'd formulated together.

"I appreciate your strategy. However, we shall bring my plans to fruition by week's end," Lord Hideaki proposed.

"Undoubtedly, Chichi-ue," Yoshinori responded, his voice a measured blend of deference and slight disappointment.

Yet, as Yoshinori began to head off to the adjacent camps, Hideaki's hand trapped his arm, halting him in his tracks.

His gaze, however, remained distantly fixed upon the horizon, his voice dropping to a sinister murmur. "Guard against overconfidence, Yoshi, and never forget that while you may command this army, it is I who command you all."

Yoshinori's eyes flared with a fusion of anger and disbelief, and he forcefully disengaged his arm from his father's clasp. Meeting Hideaki's penetrating stare with equal intensity, he spoke with venom. "Such subversion has never been my intent, nor shall it ever be." His voice held the steadiness of a running stream.

Yoshinori's footsteps reverberated with purpose as he navigated toward the other tents, intent on readying the warriors for the forthcoming day—a day destined to be filled with reconnaissance and unyielding defense tactics.

Two weeks slipped by as days melded into nights, and nights gave way to new dawns. Despite Hideaki's meticulously crafted strategies and innovative tactics, the Iron Hideaki Bushi still faced staunch resistance in Mikawa. Initially, Hideaki's strategy of covert nocturnal assaults and superior weaponry had yielded a fleeting advantage.

But the sheer size of Mikawa's forces, bolstered by the shadowy presence of Tokugawa's stealthy warriors, had effectively turned the tides, resulting in an impasse neither side had anticipated.

During the Iron Hideaki Bushi reloading of muskets, Mikawa's vast army had retaliated fiercely in the short, vulnerable span.

Like a relentless tidal wave, they descended with a barrage of flashing swords and a hail of arrows darkening the sky. The contrast was stark: the slow, methodical pace of reloading muskets against the swift, unyielding onslaught of traditional weapons.

Yoshinori watched the disarray before him. The inconsistency of their war efforts stood glaring against the backdrop of brave men fighting valiantly. A growing conviction took root in his heart: the strategy he had crafted weeks ago might be the missing piece to tilt the scales in their favor. For if it didn't, Yoshinori feared nothing else could. Then, with calculated intent, Yoshinori ordered a third of the Bushi to retreat and make their way toward Totomi.

As planned, this strategy would deceive Tokugawa into thinking that Mikawa had lost its allure for the Hideaki forces.

He also understood that as powerful as the muskets were, their limitations were evident. The long intervals to reload continuously exposed them to Mikawa's relentless assault.

This recognition was the clarion call to return to the trusted and swift traditions of Japanese martial combat.

The realization wasn't just strategic; it was also personal.

As a maestro of the blade, he knew the heart of their defense and offense lay in the sharpened edge of a samurai's sword.

Yoshinori was eager to take the lead in this dance of swift blades versus cumbersome firearms, carving a path through the adversary's flesh with the precision and swiftness only a master swordsman could muster. However, the many squandered opportunities pressed heavily on Yoshinori's heart.

Every furrow on his brow and every tense line of his lips betrayed mounting vexation, and his warriors could see it. While they had executed Lord Hideaki's tactics with precision, Yoshinori's strategy, which he believed to be their salvation, still lay dormant.

Determined to alter their course, Yoshinori decided it was time to confront his father and drive forth the final act of their grand scheme. Swiftly, he mounted his horse, its hooves beating down upon the blood-soaked earth. The chilling sight of fallen soldiers, their armor stained and faces forever frozen in their last moments, lay scattered around him.

Their silent witness only fueled Yoshinori's urgency.

CHAPTER SEVEN

Deceit's Shadow

(偽りの影)

As the sun retreated from the ravaged land, Yoshinori knew much of the day would be spent before he could rendezvous with his father at the main encampment. But time was a luxury they could no longer afford, every moment counting.

Several of Yoshinori's loyal bushi offered to escort him to the main encampment. He respectfully declined, believing that traveling lighter and faster was the essence. With the raw urgency driving him, Yoshinori's steed thundered across the landscape, hooves beating a relentless rhythm to echo his racing heart.

However, a sudden, unsettling silhouette on the horizon stopped him cold. As he drew nearer, the vague figures crystallized into four distinct shapes—men, their postures unmistakably confrontational.

They turned sharply, alerted by the rapid drumming of Yoshinori's horse's hooves. In that split second, he attempted to swerve to give himself a moment of rest and assess the situation. But they had seen him, and their intent was apparent.

They closed the gap with alarming speed.

Recognition dawned as the emblem of the Mikawa adorned their armor. *Can they discern who I am?* Yoshinori thought. But there was no time to ponder on it. Though doubt might have briefly flickered in his mind, fear had no dominion over his heart.

He stood ready to clash with any foe daring to cross his path.

And fate had thrown him into the crucible, for the soldiers were now encircling him like a pack of wolves closing in on their prey. With no time to spare, Yoshinori dismounted and sought refuge between two towering trees. The natural barrier lent him a slight advantage, partially obstructing the men's line of sight.

An almost palpable silence blanketed the area, broken only by the ominous crunching of leaves beneath the Mikawa soldiers' boots as they advanced. With a deliberate motion, Yoshinori unsheathed his blade, its polished edge gleaming menacingly, as though speaking of the countless battles witnessed. His eyes, ablaze with the fire of a thousand suns, met those of his opponents.

"A choice lies before you," declared Yoshinori, his voice echoing the confidence emanating from every fiber of his being. "Choose wisely, for this confrontation has but two outcomes."

His words were frozen in the air, unanswered as the soldiers tightened their encirclement. Then, in a flash of rage, one of the Mikawa men broke rank and charged toward Yoshinori.

However, in a graceful yet deadly arc, Yoshinori's sword met the attacker's neck, promptly decapitating him, the heavy head thudding to the earth. The hush of the woods was now punctuated by the dreadful sight and sound of the still rolling head, which came to a stop at the feet of the remaining warriors.

With a smug smile playing on his lips and blood dripping from his sword, Yoshinori addressed the remaining soldiers.

"This is your fate should you choose to remain loyal to Mikawa. Yet, a choice remains. Cast aside your emblems and fight under the banner of the Iron Hideaki Bushi, and you will stand on the right side of history."

In that charged silence, the men exchanged glances, the heavy load of Yoshinori's ultimatum weighing down their shoulders.

Then, one of the Mikawa men stepped forward, the grip on his sword tightening.

"Your offer holds no sway over me," he spat defiantly. "The man you've slain might have been the most vulnerable amongst us, so be assured, I'm not such a man. I'd rather fall in honor than serve in your shackled ranks. Your journey ends here, my friend."

The air grew colder with tension.

Yoshinori boldly replied, his voice dripping with calm audacity, "So be it. If it is death you seek, I shall dutifully oblige."

Without another word, the warriors inched closer.

Outnumbered, Yoshinori's instincts kicked in.

With a precise motion, he swept his foot across the forest floor, sending a cloud of dust and dirt flying into the faces of his aggressors. The two nearest him were caught off guard, their eyes stinging, their vision momentarily obscured.

Seizing the advantage, Yoshinori lunged forward with lightning speed, his blade slashing through the air to find its mark on one warrior, striking him to the forest ground.

As he aimed for the second adversary, the man's reflexes proved keen. He ducked in the nick of time, inadvertently causing Yoshinori's blade to lodge deep into the bark of a towering tree.

The shrill screech of steel against wood echoed hauntingly.

With a grunt of exertion, Yoshinori pulled at his weapon, freeing it just as the second warrior, his eyes now clear, charged.

Their blades sang in the stillness, each strike and block showing off their skill and training. The constant clashing was becoming, second by second, a desperate song of survival.

All the while, Yoshinori's senses remained alert, anticipating the third warrior's intervention. But mysteriously, he remained an observer, standing sentinel. Capitalizing on a moment of overextension by his adversary, Yoshinori skillfully sidestepped and, with an elegant flourish, struck a fatal blow, impaling the second man.

Blood dripped from Yoshinori's blade, the rhythmic *pat-pat* sound resonating against the silent foliage beneath.

Regaining his composure, Yoshinori shifted his gaze to the third warrior. "You've been patient. Are you awaiting a formal invitation?"

Without uttering a word, a smirk crossed the man's face as he unsheathed his blade, a unique fire burning in his eyes, different from the others. Cold, discerning, and intense, he began circling Yoshinori.

After a labored silence, the warrior finally voiced, "I wanted to see if you were worth my time."

He spoke with a chilling calmness.

"I trust I've met your expectations," Yoshinori countered.

The two samurai slowly circled each other, predators gauging the opportune moment to pounce.

Yoshinori's voice suddenly grew colder, his words sharpening as they sliced through the air. "Ending your life will bring me unique satisfaction. But fear not, for your severed head will have the honor of gracing the entrance to my castle, a grim herald leading the parade of the finest trophies I've amassed throughout the years."

Moments before their swords met, the warrior drew forth his wakizashi, pairing it with his katana, revealing his expertise in the revered art of Niten Ichi-ryū.

A shadow of a smirk touched Yoshinori's lips.

"So, you're a practitioner of the two-sword technique," he remarked, his voice dripping with casual disdain. "Such arts won't faze me." Memories of his childhood training against the masters of Niten Ichi-ryū flooded back, filling him with a fierce confidence.

Their eyes met once more, reflecting equal focus. The forest held its breath, its leaves silenced, and birds still as if nature itself stood awaiting the contest's outcome.

Yoshinori adjusted his grip on his katana and lunged at his adversary with a roar. But the man, with the grace of a dancing leaf in the wind, met his strike with both swords.

The clash of steel that ensued sent sparks flying in every direction as their blades flashed and sang. The symphony of their duel resonated throughout the woods, rendering every ground-dwelling creature silent but sending a thousand birds fleeing through the sky.

Both warriors read each other's intent and predicted every move. Yoshinori's blade aimed for the man's neck, only to be deflected by the swift motion of the wakizashi. In return, the man's katana arched toward Yoshinori, who dodged it with a desperate heave.

Suddenly, with a swift move, the man knocked Yoshinori's katana from his grasp. But, ever agile, Yoshinori rolled away from the impending wakizashi thrust that would otherwise have been his end.

He quickly rebounded, retrieving his blade.

Spotting a nearby mound, he vaulted from its height, using the momentum to launch a furious overhead strike. Their swords met in a loud clash, the shockwave rustling the surrounding foliage.

The two fighters, now visibly fatigued, their clothing torn, and bodies adorned with nicks and cuts, stared each other down.

Their breathing was ragged but their spirits still unyielding.

With a final, valiant effort, Yoshinori feinted with a low strike, diverting the man's wakizashi and, in a split second, he swept his katana upwards, disarming his opponent. But as the warrior's weapons clattered to the ground, Yoshinori pressed the tip of his blade to the man's neck but did not strike.

Instead, he extended a hand, admiration in his eyes.

"You fight with the heart of a lion," Yoshinori panted. "Such skill should not be wasted in death. Stand by my side as my Yōnin steward, and together, we shall carve our own legacy, making us an invincible force. Help us bring Mikawa under our dominion, and you shall be awarded lands aplenty, along with coffers filled to the brim."

The wounded man, now propped on one elbow, gasped for breath as he processed the scale of Yoshinori's proposition.

His mind was in turmoil as he clutched at the searing pain radiating from his wounds.

"How can I be assured of your loyalty? How do I know you won't dispose of me the moment Mikawa falls into your hands?" the man challenged, his voice barely above a whisper.

Yoshinori's eyes showed danger and promise. He responded, "In truth, you cannot. But should my intention have been to rid myself of you, be certain that I would have taken advantage of your present vulnerability and concluded our duel with your bloody death."

With his hand still extended, Yoshinori gestured for the man to retake it. With a hesitation speaking of much internal conflict, the man finally raised his hand to meet Yoshinori's.

"You have made a wise decision," Yoshinori declared as he assisted the man to his feet. The two retrieved their steeds, rummaging through their pouches to produce rags, soon to wipe away the mix of blood and sweat from their visages.

"Come," commanded Yoshinori, excitement lining his voice. "We must meet with my chichi-ue to devise our strategy. With your intimate knowledge of the Mikawa warriors, victory will swiftly follow, and an abundant wealth will be yours for the taking."

The men mounted their horses, the steeds stamping impatiently, ready to embark on their journey.

The man's eyes dropped to the lifeless forms of his former comrades, their bodies now partially obscured by the rustling leaves that had begun to claim them. A pang of sorrow pricked at his heart.

Noticing the melancholy that seemed to cloud the man's demeanor, Yoshinori sought to pierce through the gloom.

He offered rare words of reassurance.

"What is your name, warrior?" questioned Yoshinori.

The man hesitated momentarily before responding, "My name is Katsuro."

"Do not let your heart be burdened by the dead, Katsuro," Yoshinori advised, his tone embodying an air of stoicism. "They have fulfilled their destiny, and we shall go forward to fulfill ours."

The passage of hours was imperceptible as Yoshinori and Katsuro spurred their steeds onward. Yoshinori, driven by the need to recoup precious moments squandered in combat, was wary of the encroaching dusk. The falling darkness might embolden hidden Mikawa warriors to intercept them, a risk that could sway Katsuro's nascent loyalty if he were outnumbered. With a strategic mind, Yoshinori had Katsuro lead the way, a tactful move to keep the man within his sight without raising suspicion.

As the final hues of daylight retreated, the intimidating silhouette of Lord Hideaki's encampment loomed into view.

Warriors from the bushi, with hands on hilts and suspicion in their eyes, greeted them with an air of hostility as they scrutinized Katsuro.

Both men disembarked with measured calm, but the atmosphere was thick with an unspoken animosity. Katsuro, confronted by the steely glances of men honing their blades and training with muskets, felt an unease settle within him. Then, a foul scent drifted to him, the stench of scorched flesh from afar, bringing a lump to his throat.

Would it have been more honorable to fall by the sword? Katsuro questioned himself silently, considering his uncertain future.

Inside the tent, a fire crackled, flickering shadows claiming the space as Lord Hideaki sat in deep concentration.

Maps and scrolls were strewn before him, each marking the lifeblood of strategies yet to unfold.

His eyes did not stray from the parchments as the men entered.

Hideaki's voice, laced with irritation, cut through the warmth. "Why are you here, Yoshi?" he demanded without preamble.

Yoshinori, undeterred, spoke with urgency. "Lord Chichi-ue, time is a luxury we no longer possess. I've come to repropose my strategy of a feint toward Totomi. Our current strategy leaves us vulnerable, and our muskets cannot be reloaded swiftly enough to prevent a massacre," he explained.

The question from Hideaki was pointed and practical.

"And why not send a courier or a messenger with such news? Why do you gamble with your safety?"

Yoshinori's reply was well considered, his eyes locking with his father's. "A messenger relays information, whereas my presence here signifies the gravity of our situation. This matter demands our immediate and undivided attention."

Hideaki paused, his scrutinizing gaze shifting to Katsuro, taking in the sight of the man still bearing the symbols of Mikawa.

The air grew taut as his eyes narrowed, the disdain in his voice unmistakable. "Yoshi, explain yourself. What compels you to sully my quarters with this Mikawa cur?"

Katsuro, sensing the animosity, swiftly stripped away the remnants of his former allegiance, discarding the Mikawa insignia as if he were a viper shedding an old skin.

" Chichi-ue, this is Katsuro. His defection turns the tides in our favor. With his intimate knowledge of Mikawa's defenses, we will breach their walls and set our sights on Totomi with unprecedented speed."

Hideaki's lips curled into a sneer, his tone edged in skepticism.

"He stands unslain, which suggests he posed a considerable challenge. Did he nearly best you, son?"

Yoshinori's reply came with an edge of pride. "A formidable challenge, yes, but not an impossible one. He fought bravely, but my victory was always assured. His demise would have been a simple feat. Yet, what value is there in the death of a man whose mind holds the keys to our conquest? In life, he will serve a purpose far greater than being another corpse on the battlefield."

The room fell into a heavy silence, thick with tension.

Katsuro, feeling increasingly like a pawn in a larger game, shifted uncomfortably under these scrutinizing eyes. His thoughts raced as he contemplated his precarious situation.

Could I seize Yoshinori's sword in time to defend myself? Even if it meant a swift death, it would be an honorable end, he mused.

But before he could further entertain these thoughts, Lord Hideaki's voice swept through the silence like a hurricane.

"What does he gain from this?" Hideaki inquired, his eyes still fixed on Katsuro.

Yoshinori answered firmly, "I have promised him war spoils, a new home, and wealth beyond measure."

Hideaki considered this for a moment, his gaze piercing. "Very well," he finally declared with an obvious staunchness.

"Yoshi, if your strategy plays out as planned, the shogun's forces will be drawn to defend Totomi, leaving Mikawa vulnerable. We will rally our warriors using Katsuro's insider knowledge to identify their key defenses. With the ferocity of a storm, we will seize Mikawa, completing our conquest."

Hideaki's scrutinizing gaze lingered on Katsuro, his voice dripping with animosity. "You better keep your newfound dog in check, Yoshinori. The consequences will be severe if I detect any hint of betrayal or cowardice."

Yoshinori's response was firm, "Understood, Chichi-ue. Should the need arise, I will take the necessary actions myself."

Amidst this verbal volley, Katsuro's patience frayed. Stepping forward, he injected a firm edge into his voice. "Enough! You speak as though I am not here. I chose this path willingly. Now, let us focus on what's important: our strategy for victory."

Hideaki raised an eyebrow, a slight amusement in his tone.

"Your new dog shows courage, Yoshinori." A grudging respect in his voice, he continued, "He's right. Let's get to the heart of our plan."

Throughout the night in the battle tent, shadows danced in time with the flickering candlelight.

Lord Hideaki Yoshinori, alongside Katsuro, sat scrutinizing the maps of Mikawa. The weight of impending battle and the faint scent of ink and parchment filled the air.

Katsuro, having turned his back on his warriors, now divulged their secrets to Lord Hideaki and Yoshinori.

"My Lord," Katsuro began, his voice steady yet tinged with a deep tension, "this thicket, here, serves as our covert bastion from whence we shall launch our ambushes."

His finger traced the dense forests and hidden valleys of Mikawa, lands he had once called home, now turned into a stage for betrayal.

With each location he pointed out, a piece of Katsuro's resolve crumbled, yet he continued.

"And here," he indicated, "is where we time the reload of your bushi's muskets, a moment of vulnerability crucial to your strategy."

Then, his hand hovered over specific sites on the map, revealing the location of the Horokubiya ceramics.

"These are no ordinary vessels," Katsuro explained, his voice displaying a frisson of reluctant admiration. "When ignited, the Horokubiyas rupture with a force fierce enough to shatter the bushi ranks. The Horokubiya are why this siege has been going on for seven years; they are our hidden dragons, lying in wait."

As he spoke, turmoil churned within Katsuro.

A lump of anxiety was swelling in his throat, as bulky as a melon. These were his fellow countrymen he was betraying, warriors he'd once fought alongside.

As a child, a similar situation had also taken place.

The memory of his lost family—his mother, father, and two brothers, whose lives had been extinguished during Nobunaga's ruthless rise in Edo—haunted him. Their loss did not quell the sense of treachery now consuming his soul.

Lord Hideaki, observing Katsuro's inner conflict, addressed him in a tone that balanced the demands of war with a note of empathy that even surprised Yoshinori.

"Katsuro, the burden of loyalty is often laden with sacrifice. As promised by Yoshi, your dedication in this dire hour, despite the ghosts of your past, will not be forgotten."

Katsuro bowed his head, silently acknowledging his new daimyo's words. The dawn was creeping in, bringing a cool, pale light into the tent, heralding a day of confrontation to come.

Katsuro steeled himself, pushing aside the shadows of betrayal and focusing on the strategy laid out before them.

After only a few hours of restless repose, the dawn bore witness to a grim scene. Katsuro, alongside the powerful Iron Hideaki Bushi, launched their assault on the strategic hideouts of the Mikawa forces. This attack, orchestrated by Lord Hideaki, was executed with a ruthless ferocity that spared none, not even women and children.

The sky was colored with ominous hues of destruction as villages succumbed to flames, their smoky tendrils rising like wraiths against the morning light.

Amid this chaos, Katsuro was moving almost like a specter, his actions on the battlefield lacking their usual precision.

His swordplay, ordinarily a dance of deadly grace, had grown erratic and unfocused. Each swing of his blade, each life he extinguished, added weight to the turmoil wracking his conscience.

His head hung heavy, not with the exhaustion of battle but rather with the unbearable burden of his betrayal.

Far to the west of Mikawa, the main contingent of the Iron Bushi under Yoshinori's strategic command, had executed their plan flawlessly. The Tokugawa forces, deceived by their maneuver, had redirected their might toward Totomi. This diversion exposed Mikawa, its defense now reliant solely on local warriors. These fighters, once unstoppable in their guerilla tactics, had found their effectiveness crippled in the wake of Katsuro's treachery.

The landscape of Mikawa, once thrumming with the spirited resistance of its local warriors, now lay entombed in a harrowing silence, broken only by the crackling of fires and the distant clangs of the Iron Hideaki Bushi's unrelenting advance.

The strategic brilliance of Yoshinori had paved the way for a crushing blow, but it was Katsuro's betrayal that had sealed the fate of Mikawa, leaving its heart exposed and its villages all in ruin.

In this moment of conquest and devastation, Katsuro's soul was ensnared in a battle far more torturous than the physical conflicts around. His internal strife mirrored his homeland's smoldering ruins, a poignant reminder of the harrowing cost of war and betrayal.

CHAPTER EIGHT

The Harbinger

(予兆者)

As the final traces of winter began to recede, it became clear that Chiyo had seamlessly woven herself into the fabric of Amara's family. Each morning, she would join Amara and Yasuke in their rituals of training and meditation, an integral part of their daily life.

Yasuke, despite his reservations about Amara having slain her first enemy at such a tender age, was committed to training Chiyo too.

His belief was resolute: the girls must be able to defend themselves. Yasuke, once a relentless warrior under Oda Nobunaga, and known for his ruthless battle brutality, harbored a deep conviction, wanting to instill in the two girls a sense that resorting to bloodshed was not the sole path. This was, of course, in stark contrast to his bloodstained legacy under Nobunaga.

Amara, who had shown considerable restraint at the beginning of her confrontation, only to ultimately take a life in self-defense, was a case in point for Yasuke's philosophy. However, Yasuke had sensed a profound transformation in her since that fateful night. Her complexity and unreadable demeanor were becoming more apparent; even Yuki, ever observant, felt this profound change in Amara.

On a serene evening, just as the setting sun afforded its glow to the landscape, Amara and Chiyo wrapped up their training session.

The air was filled with the tranquility of the golden hour, a stark contrast to the rigors of their practice.

"That was an excellent session," Chiyo remarked, a light confidence in her voice due to her newly acquired skills. She was looking forward to the relief that awaited at the house. "I can't wait to get back and rest."

Amara, however, had other plans.

"Then you go ahead without me," she said, "I will be down in a few hours."

Taken aback by Amara's response, Chiyo couldn't mask her surprise. "What are you saying? I am confused."

Amara's reply was unyielding, her words showing an intensity reflecting inner turmoil. She was nowhere near ready to rest.

"I am never done," she stated, slicing her katana through the air.

The air hung still for a moment, punctuated only by the gentle rustling of branches swaying in the wind. Chiyo's voice abruptly broke this brief interlude of calm. "Well, if you're staying, I'm staying too," she declared, defiance embedded in her words.

Amara, shocked, looked at Chiyo with a side glance.

"Really?" she asked with astonishment and gratitude.

Chiyo's response was heartfelt. "We're sisters; you convinced your family to take me in when my own abandoned me, casting me aside like trash on the streets. Why would I choose to separate from you?"

Moved by Chiyo's loyalty and the depth of their bond, Amara closed the distance between them and embraced her tightly. "Yes, we are sisters, and we will always protect each other," she affirmed.

Then Amara's demeanor shifted abruptly, mirroring the erratic nature of the wind. Her voice now carried a more searing intensity.

"I … no … *we* must grow stronger, more formidable. After my encounter with my uncle's men and hearing my father's tales over the years, I've learned this world harbors no kindness at all for the weak.

"My father became a beast to contend with beasts. Why should we, as women, temper our own strength?"

Her words were a genuine outpouring of conviction.

Ever the embodiment of tranquility, Chiyo sought to soothe the storm in Amara's heart. "But you cannot equate your journey with your father's," she implored gently. "He served under the merciless Nobunaga, forced to commit acts and transform into someone he never wished to be, all to ensure his survival."

"And where did that lead him?" Amara interjected, her voice demonstrating both anger and pain. "To years of fleeing and hiding. And you, your skin is of this land. Yet, see how they sneer and jeer in the marketplace. For years, I've pretended their taunts about my dark skin don't wound me …"

She paused, much hurt evident in her expression.

"They will never cease until they grow weary and seek to expel the foreign 'beast' from their midst."

The turmoil within Amara was reaching a boiling point, and Chiyo could see that the once-composed warrior was struggling to maintain her balance. She had noticed a change in Amara's routine too; the peaceful practice of meditation was increasingly being replaced by relentless swordplay and karate.

Chiyo reached out, grasping Amara's hand with a gentle firmness.

"Listen, we will train harder daily, as you wish," Chiyo soothingly proposed. "But let's also focus on meditation and reflection. I promise to stay by your side and never leave if we commit to this."

Chiyo had an innate understanding of Amara's troubles and seemed to know precisely how to address them. Her suggestion was not just a compromise but a lifeline, offering Amara a way to channel her turmoil into something healing and grounding.

Back at home, Yuki was immersed in the familiar rhythms of preparing supper, her hands deftly moving amidst an array of fresh ingredients. The aroma of the evening meal filled the air, weaving a comforting energy within the walls of their home. Meanwhile, Yasuke was away, bartering with locals in the community for provisions and materials to further enhance their small property.

Over the years, the once dilapidated house had been transformed into a dwelling of both function and beauty.

Under Yasuke's skilled hands and with the help of Yuki and the girls, the home had been carefully restored. Every crevice had been sealed too, protecting its inhabitants from the relentless pursuit of insects and the harshness of the elements.

Yasuke had not only expanded the living space but had also realized his vision of a complete dojo. He had carefully partitioned multiple rooms, equipping each with wooden and cloth fusuma sliding panels, ensuring privacy and tranquility for the girls.

During the warmer months, the interior and exterior alike were adorned with vibrant flowers from Yuki's meticulously tended garden. The home's beauty had not gone unnoticed by the neighboring community, often leading them to seek Yasuke's expertise in designing their own home improvements.

As Yuki stirred the pot, her gaze drifted to the window, catching the silhouette of a figure approaching.

Too early for Yasuke's return, she thought, her curiosity piqued.

She opened the door with a sense of intrigue, only to be met by the unexpected sight of her brother, Hideyoshi.

A torrent of emotions cascaded through Yuki at the sight of him. Years had passed since their last unpleasant encounter, their communication severed except for sporadic, often unsettling news of his confrontations with Amara and Chiyo in the marketplace.

Yuki's mind was racing with possibilities.

Was Hideyoshi here to reconcile after all these years or to offer apologies for his men's recent misconduct?

As she stepped closer, the initial flicker of a smile on her face transformed into a look of deep concern.

Hideyoshi's look was not one of reconciliation, but rather, it was twisted in a simmering rage.

The air around them thickened, hinting at the storm of confrontation that was looming on their horizon.

In a menacing tone, Hideyoshi broke the uneasy silence.

"I demand to know, where is that abomination you call a daughter? If you had any sense, you, the foreigner, and your kuroi hada child would flee Yamazato. My worker, Saburo, informed me of Amara and your men's actions against Koichi. When his family seeks justice, I will direct them to you without hesitation or regret."

Yuki, undaunted, met his hostility with a calm, almost sarcastic smile. She stepped closer to Hideyoshi, her movements poised and deliberate. "Oh, dear brother, you are mistaken. There were no men. Only Amara bested your worker. Times have changed since Father and the community cast us to the outskirts of Yamazato."

Her voice was imbued with a calm, unyielding strength.

As Yuki circled Hideyoshi, her eyes locked with his.

The intensity in his gaze did not falter, but Yuki continued, undeterred. "My family and I will not abandon our home or land to your threats," she declared. "We are not afraid of your sort."

Hideyoshi spat back, "Father and I always knew you were foolish, but this … this is madness beyond anything I imagined."

"Get off my land!" Yuki demanded, her tone now forceful and commanding.

"Or what?" Hideyoshi challenged, his disdain evident.

"Or I will have Yasuke scatter pieces of you across Yamazato." Yuki retorted with a boldness that seemed to take Hideyoshi aback.

This new Yuki was a far cry from the timid girl he remembered.

In a sudden surge of anger, Hideyoshi raised his hand to strike her. But Yuki, with a grace borne of necessity, deftly sidestepped his blow and positioned herself behind him as if taunting him.

With the kitchen knife she had been using for lunch now drawn from her apron, Yuki seized Hideyoshi by the ponytail of his chonmage hairstyle, pressing the blade to his jawline.

"I told you, dear brother, times have changed. Neither you, nor anyone else, will ever intimidate me again. Now leave!" She sent him staggering in the opposite direction with one forceful, hefty shove.

Yuki's assertive behavior was not just uncharacteristic of her; it also overtly defied the typical expectations of a woman from Yamazato. Yuki was right, and this sudden and bold defiance left Hideyoshi grappling with the stark realization that his sister had undergone some sort of profound transformation.

In his mind, there could be only one explanation for such a change: Yasuke.

What kind of man allows this behavior from women, shaping Amara and Yuki into figures so starkly different from the conventional women of our locality?

Hideyoshi pondered, confusion and resentment brewing.

Regaining his balance, Hideyoshi made his way back to his horse, his pride bruised and his mind swirling with unsettled thoughts.

Reluctantly approaching his steed, he caught sight of Amara and Chiyo descending the hill, their training session having concluded.

Their presence only fueled his simmering anger.

Hideyoshi fixed his eyes on Amara with a gaze as scorching as the midsummer sun. The disdain in his look was profound, and under his breath, he muttered the word "beast."

The venom in his voice was barely a whisper, yet it carried the burdensome cargo of his many deep-seated prejudices and hatred.

This moment was more than a mere confrontation between siblings; it was a clash of old values against new, of a past refusing to yield to the unfolding realities of the infiltrating present.

Hideyoshi, rooted in the traditions of their community, found himself confounded by the boldness and strength that Yasuke had instilled in his family. As he mounted his horse and rode away,

Hideyoshi thought, *what if this will become the new norm for women here? That dark foreigner must be dealt with.*

Amara and Chiyo wasted no time, dashing toward Yuki with urgency. Amara was frustrated, her voice reflecting annoyance as she asked, "What did that man want?"

"Nothing," Yuki responded briefly, trying to dismiss the matter.

Amara, not easily convinced, pressed on.

"Okāsan, please!" she insisted, knowing there was more to the story.

Sensing the girls' persistence, Yuki gave in.

"He claimed he came to warn us, but it was veiled as a threat, as is typical with my brother," Yuki explained with exasperation. "He said the family of the man you confronted with your blade will seek retribution and that he will support them. He demanded that we leave and didn't appreciate my refusal."

Amara's expression turned steely. "Whether his threats have any real substance or not, we will not abandon our home," she stated.

"No, we will not," Yuki agreed with equal determination. "Now, come girls, let's finish preparing the meal. Your chichi-ue will be returning soon."

A short time later, the sound of a familiar footfall approached the house as the kitchen filled with the warmth of the afternoon meal preparations. Yasuke, having spent the day assisting locals with renovations, returned home, his hands bearing the fruits of his labor.

He had become well-known in the community for his skill in crafting and repairing homes, a talent he often traded for wood and essential supplies. The sound of his footsteps on the gravel path comforted Yuki, signaling his imminent presence.

Yasuke entered the home, the aroma of cooking greeting him like an old friend. "The joy of returning home to you ladies and to a warm meal never diminishes," he remarked with a contented smile, setting down the wood and supplies he had acquired. As Yasuke washed his hands, ready to join in the evening's meal preparations, Yuki approached him, her steps measured, a subtle tension beneath her calm exterior. As they moved together toward the table, her mind was a rush of thought, contemplating the right moment to disclose her brother's unsettling visit. She decided to wait, allowing Yasuke the comfort of the meal and some moments of rest before burdening him with the day's troubling events.

Amara, however, carried a different wish. Recently, she had grown more accustomed to confronting challenges head-on, a trait shining brightly in her character. Observing her mother's hesitation, Amara decided to reveal the news herself.

Her intention was not to defy Yuki but was driven by a desire to address the looming threat without delay, to cut through the unease that had been permeating the air since Hideyoshi's departure.

Amara's eyes blazed with frustration. " Chichi-ue, that wretched uncle of mine visited while you were out."

Yasuke, in the midst of his meal, paused, a piece of saba fish halfway to his mouth. He swallowed hastily, his eyes darting toward Yuki as he set down his chopsticks.

"Why did he come here?" Yasuke inquired, his voice steady.

Yuki, giving a disapproving glance at Amara for her abruptness, answered, "He came under the guise of a warning or perhaps a threat. The family of the man Amara killed is influential, and my brother indicated he would direct them to us."

Yasuke's expression hardened slightly. "Your brother has never shown concern for our welfare; his words were undoubtedly a threat." After a brief, contemplative silence, he asked calmly, "Was there more to his visit?"

"Yes," Yuki admitted, showing defiance and concern. "He reacted poorly to my response, and when he raised his hand to strike me, I defended myself with my kitchen knife. I fear my reaction alone may spur him to lead the slain man's family right to our doorstep."

A heavy silence fell over the room, but Yasuke's face remained impassive, falling into the pattern of his usual unshakeable demeanor. Known for his stoic resolve even during his time leading Nobunaga's bushi, his unwavering calm had often been the pillar bolstering the spirits of his men in the face of daunting challenges.

Breaking the silence, Yasuke declared, "I will go to the heart of the settlement tomorrow and confront Hideyoshi. My approach will not be one of malice but of reason."

His voice, resolute yet devoid of anger, reflected a strategy of confrontation, diplomacy, and strength.

"Do you truly believe that to be wise?" Yuki questioned.

Yasuke pondered for a moment. "Perhaps not. But neither is it wise to await their next move."

Amara's spirit was unquenched by the gravity of the situation; she chimed in, "Could Chiyo and I accompany you?"

"No," Yasuke answered with firm finality.

"But … but … we can help!" Amara protested.

Yasuke remained firm. "No, you must assist your mother with the chores. More importantly, you must stay and safeguard our home."

His directive was not just a command but a strategy, ensuring their home remained fortified and functioning in his absence. Amara silently nodded in agreement, understanding that Yasuke's decisions were unchangeable due to his deep-seated wisdom and experience.

As dawn broke, a gentle light covered the land, the tranquil morning air carrying the sound of Yasuke meticulously preparing his horse. The steady brush strokes against the animal's coat and carefully removing debris from its hooves created a calm yet purposeful atmosphere.

Yasuke continued his preparations, offering the horse millet and water for the journey ahead. Amara, her feet bare and eyes still heavy with sleep, approached him urgently in the stable. "Are you sure you don't want me to accompany you?" she asked, her voice tinged with a barely restrained anger. "You're quite sure?"

Yasuke remained silent, continuing his task of feeding the horse.

Amara, persistent, pleaded, "I won't be in the way. Chiyo is strong, and she can help Mother defend our home. It's unlikely anyone would dare attack us here."

Finally, Yasuke responded while checking the horse's stirrups and bridle. "My dear daughter," he began, "you have grown beyond my expectations in skill and strength. Yet, I sense a dangerous eagerness for conflict within you."

"No, Chichi-ue! I … I …" Amara attempted to interject, but Yasuke's stern eye stopped her short.

"I taught you long ago that true strength and power do not reside in the act of killing but rather in the ability to protect and show restraint. Every life, even an enemy's, holds value. Taking a life must always be a last resort." Yasuke's voice was heavy with wisdom.

He exhaled a deep, meaningful sigh.

Yasuke then sheathed his sword, Kurokaze, glancing thoughtfully at Amara. Her words were ready to spill out, her frustration palpable.

"I understand life's value and do not wish to take it lightly. But these people will not cease their hostility. They despise us. They despise our dark skin, Chichi-ue," Amara said, anger simmering.

"Are you not also going with the intent to fight and kill, Chichi-ue? That's why you have Kurokaze, isn't it?" she accused.

Yasuke, slowly mounting his horse, paused to take Amara's hand.

"As a samurai, and as you become one, we are bound by duty and honor. Our role is not to seek conflict but to maintain peace, to serve our family with integrity, and to use our skills for the greater good. Kurokaze shall defend, just as you will also. From here."

As he began to leave the stable, the sun climbing higher, Yasuke looked back and added, "I once served my Damiyo in battles that required me to take many lives. Whether for revenge or duty, killing leaves a lasting scar on the soul. It can ignite a cycle of vengeance that affects not just you, but also entire families and communities."

Then Amara, with a sad stare at Yasuke, stated, "I don't feel anything for the man I killed. Is that wrong?"

She paused, waiting. No response came to that question, perhaps designed to leave her thinking. Or perhaps Father was just keen to get off, to make progress on his quest.

"I'll return soon, Amara."

His words lingered, with disappointment as he rode away, leaving Amara to ponder her words and his teachings amidst the breaking dawn.

As Amara stood in the stable, the gentle breeze weaving through her hair, self-doubt washed over her. *Does Father see me as a monster?* she wondered, the thought gnawing at her conscience.

Regret clouded Amara's mind.

She retreated from the stable, her heart heavy with the turmoil that had been simmering within her for the past few weeks.

Always obedient and respectful, this was the first time she had ever considered defying Yasuke's wishes.

Resolved to act, Amara quietly dressed, intent on going to the marketplace to support her father, ignoring what he had said.

She moved stealthily across the creaking wooden floor, reaching for her katana, trying not to disturb Yuki. Katana in hand, she tiptoed toward the door, only to be halted by a firm grip on her forearm.

It was so strong that it rooted her to the spot.

"I look up to you," whispered a voice from the shadows. Chiyo's face emerged, illuminated by sun rays slicing through the window. "Don't make this about you. Our father—your father—told us to stay here to protect our home. That's what we must do," Chiyo insisted.

A heavy silence enveloped the room.

Amara stood frozen, aware that Chiyo, despite her courage, was no match for her. Yet the fact that Chiyo was willing to risk their friendship to uphold Yasuke's directive spoke volumes. A pang of sadness touched Amara's heart as she looked at Chiyo.

"You're right, my dear friend … my sister," Amara conceded, her voice softening. "I just want to ensure he's safe and protect him."

"Yasuke is among the most intimidating samurai this land has ever known," Chiyo reminded her. "It would take a hundred warriors just to slow him down."

A smile of reassurance crept across Amara's face, easing the tension in her posture. "So, what should we do with all these emotions?" she asked, giggling and her spirit lightening.

"Let's meditate and train," Chiyo suggested, guiding them back to their foundational practices of discipline and focus.

Amara nodded, reflecting their unity.

Without wasting another moment, Chiyo turned and rushed to change into her training attire, the house now fallen into silence except for the soft rustle of movement.

Soon, Chiyo reappeared at the door, now dressed and prepared. Her eyes met Amara's, demonstrating a shared purpose.

"Shall we?" Amara asked, extending her hand as an invitation to a shared journey of camaraderie.

Chiyo's hand found Amara's in a firm clasp.

As one, they moved, their steps mirroring each other's. The morning air, fresh and crisp, welcomed them.

Meanwhile, as Yasuke emerged from the shadowy embrace of the forest, the bustling marketplace of Yamazato was also coming into view. The journey had given him ample time to ponder his impending confrontation with Hideyoshi. Twenty years prior, Hideyoshi would have been unable to anticipate an attack from Yasuke, much less survive a strike from Kurokaze. Nor would he have mistaken Yasuke's composed demeanor for any kind of weakness.

As Yasuke observed the marketplace, teeming with people absorbed in their daily routines, he noted that some locals were directing more glances his way than usual.

Has Hideyoshi already stirred the people into anticipating a conflict? Yasuke wondered. His gaze then fell upon Hideyoshi's stall, buzzing with patrons. He navigated through the crowd with deliberate movements, his presence parting the sea of people.

Finally, he stood directly in front of Hideyoshi's stall.

Upon noticing Yasuke, Hideyoshi momentarily froze, a flicker of shock and fear betraying his usual composure. However, he quickly masked his emotions, regaining his poise. In a bid to recover his pride, Hideyoshi raised his voice, feigning anger.

"Why are you here, sullying my space with your presence?"

Yasuke, undeterred by the outburst, replied sternly, his hand resting on the hilt of Kurokaze. "We need to talk … now."

The firmness in his voice and the subtle gesture toward his sword conveyed a dire warning.

The patrons at Hideyoshi's stall registered confusion and curiosity as they witnessed this tense exchange.

Sensing Yasuke's presence and the seriousness of his tone, Hideyoshi acquiesced to the demand with a reluctant nod.

"Very well," Hideyoshi conceded, his voice tinged with a begrudging acceptance. Turning to his patrons, he maintained a calm facade. "I shall return shortly," he informed them, his words carefully measured to conceal the undercurrent of tension.

As Hideyoshi stepped away from the stall, the murmurs among the patrons grew, their eyes flickering between the departing Hideyoshi and Yasuke. The tension was evident when the two men faced off in a secluded back alley behind the stall.

Yasuke, significantly taller and more imposing, towered over Hideyoshi. Then Yasuke reminded himself that his purpose here was not one of aggression but rather, it was to confront and understand Hideyoshi's deep-seated hatred and prejudice.

With Hideyoshi's full attention, Yasuke spoke assertively.

"In a land torn by constant war, where daimyos vie for control while innocent women and children are murdered and kidnapped in their wake, why do you, Hideyoshi, direct such intense hatred toward your kin? What fuels this disdain toward your sister?"

Yasuke's question cleaved its way through the alley's silence, seeking the root of Hideyoshi's bitterness.

Hideyoshi paused, his expression tightening.

Then he said, "My sister has always defied norms, never fitting the mold of a traditional Japanese woman. As a child, she would constantly challenge our father, especially after our mother's death. Then, her association with a foreigner was the final, unbearable insult to my father and this community." Hideyoshi's words were sharp, like arrows shot with silent, deadly intent. He had more to say.

"You came to our land as a mere slave, turned bodyguard, acting on your master's commands. You brought no status, no noble lineage, and you've diluted our heritage," Hideyoshi spat out, venom dripping from every word. Then he paused briefly, wiping his mouth before continuing with his habitually scornful tone. "Japan's strength has always been rooted in social harmony, where each person understands and fulfills their role. An outsider like you, so distinct in appearance and culture, disrupts this delicate balance."

Yasuke, not one to let such accusations go unchallenged, swiftly interjected, "I hold Japan's customs and traditions in the highest regard, which is precisely why I chose to make this land my home and raise my daughter alongside your sister. I aim to honor these traditions while introducing the richness of my own culture, believing in the strength that comes from mutual understanding."

Unswayed by Yasuke's reasoning, Hideyoshi fired back another volley of his entrenched beliefs. "Our land has thrived on the purity of our people. Introducing foreign blood, especially with those as visibly distinct as Amara, disrupts our race's purity. Japan's history was built on unity and homogeneity. I would die to preserve our traditions and the purity of our people."

Yasuke countered calmly, "My heritage, just like yours, Hideyoshi, is rich and ancient. By sharing our strengths, we do not dilute our cultures. Instead, we enhance and uplift them, weaving in greater strengths and ensuring a richer life for our future generations."

Hideyoshi's disdain for Yasuke's perspective was evident as he retorted, "Nonsense. You have no respect for our culture. Teaching women to fight is a direct insult to our traditions. Women have their roles, and men have theirs, rooted in heritage and custom.

"Everyone knows that by training women in the art of combat, you are not just flouting our customs but also, potentially sowing chaos by encouraging women to step beyond their societal roles."

As Hideyoshi's voice grew louder with conviction, Yasuke realized the futility of the argument. "I see your mind is set," he said. Then, with a stern warning, he added, "Just stay away from my family, and you will live to be an old man. That is all I have to say."

Hideyoshi's response was a derisive chuckle. "You should be more concerned about others than about me. Just last night, the family of the man your daughter killed was here, rallying people against you and your family. While you've been here confronting me, they may already be at your home, getting their vengeance."

Yasuke's expression turned from surprise to anger. "You warned your sister about this? Did you think you were helping?" he asked. "You're a bad omen, like a black kite; your very presence makes you a harbinger of death! And now, you've led them straight to our doorstep? Is that what you have done?"

"I have only spoken the truth," Hideyoshi replied smugly. "Yuki should have listened. That is all I have to say."

Infuriated, Yasuke issued a final threat.

"If my family is harmed, I'll ensure you never find peace until I've removed your head from your body. You should leave here for good, or you might regret that you didn't."

With that, Yasuke spun around, dashed to the front of the stall, mounted his horse swiftly, and galloped toward the forest.

His mind was now racing with concern for his family's safety. The urgency of the situation lent speed to his ride, each thunderous hoofbeat a race against time to protect his family.

CHAPTER NINE

Dances of Doves and Vultures

(鳩とハゲタカの舞)

Now nearing the halfway point in the sky, the sun pierced the canopy, scattering light across the forest, dispelling the chill and darkness with its warm embrace. Yet, for Yasuke, the beauty of the scene passed unnoticed. His senses were focused only on two things: the relentless pounding of his horse's hooves against the earth and the uncontrollable, forceful beating of his heart.

Yasuke, a man renowned for his unshakeable composure, found himself in the grip of an unfamiliar anxiety, slightly unseated.

The dense forest around him, usually a place of solace and contemplation, now felt like a barrier, conspiring to slow his journey.

Each thunderous gallop of his horse only indicated a desperate need to reach those he loved. His breath came in short, sharp bursts, mirroring the frantic rhythm of his horse's hooves against the earth. The usually comforting rustle of the leaves now sounded like whispers of doom, adding to his growing sense of dread.

This was a different battle, one not fought on the fields of war but within the depths of his heart, at his very own door, rooted among those he loved more than anything.

The ones he valued more than life.

Protecting his men in battle was a duty he had always performed with a calm detachment, necessary for the task. But protecting his family was a responsibility that struck at the very core of his being.

It was a protective instinct far more profound than anything he could ever experience on the battlefield, driving him forth with an intensity that bordered on an unhinged desperation.

Meanwhile, in the midst of the peaceful valley, the sharp sound of clashing swords reverberated, disrupting the peaceful ambiance.

Amara pushed Chiyo back with a slight edge in strength, a playful grin adorning her face. Chiyo, well-versed in Amara's techniques from their extensive training together, swiftly spun around, exploiting Amara's forward momentum to unbalance her slightly.

The young women paused, facing each other, their giggles echoing as they relished the strategic interplay of their training.

As they wrapped up the initial phase of their exercises, they found themselves at the crest of the valley, utterly captivated by the boundless splendor lying before them.

The breeze tenderly rustled the Japanese Cedar trees, painting a tranquil tableau extending as far as the eye could see.

Chiyo, lost in the moment, sighed wistfully. "I wish it could always be like this," she said. Her voice then became somber. "I remember my father's warnings and Yasuke's words about a warlord intent on conquering Japan, province by province. If such a thing were to happen, this beautiful land, this moment of peace, could be lost."

Ever confident and buoyed by her father's strength, Amara replied, "Well, luckily for us, my Chichi-ue won't let that happen." Her words exhibited hope and unshakable faith in Yasuke, also pride.

"Come," Amara beckoned with renewed energy, "let's meditate and reflect on our training. We had a good session, didn't we?"

Collecting their gear and sheathing their swords, the pair began their descent down the hill. They directed their steps toward the house to a nook adjacent to Yuki's garden, their usual meditation spot. In the warmer months, this secluded corner offered the lush vibrancy of Yuki's flowers. Yet, in the colder months, it still served as their sanctuary, a haven for introspection and inner tranquility amidst the unpredictability of the increasingly chaotic world beyond.

As Amara and Chiyo immersed themselves in the serenity of their meditation, unbeknownst to them, danger lurked at the forest's edge.

Tadashi, Koichi's older brother, fueled by a thirst for vengeance, had spent the night gathering a group of intimidating men.

His sole mission was to exact retribution on the family he held responsible for his brother's demise.

With each step, the grass of the forest succumbed to the advancing adversaries. Garbed in combat kimonos, each warrior moved with a silent, deadly intent. Their katanas hung at their sides, signaling their readiness for battle.

Two of the men, carrying Yari spears, trailed slightly behind, their positioning strategic and calculated. They were prepared to break away and flank the target at a moment's notice. Tadashi, a master in the art of wielding a kusarigama, led the group with a grim purpose. The chain and sickle weapon, deadly in his skilled hands, added a more menacing edge to his presence.

The other two men in the group were armed with wakizashis alongside their katanas, a combination speaking of their versatility and lethal prowess. These men, with their array of weapons and battle-hardened skills, created a formidable force, capable of swiftly overpowering anyone in their path.

Amara and Chiyo, entwined in the peaceful embrace of meditation, began the delicate process of emerging from their deep, introspective state. Their awareness gently transitioned from the serene depths of their inner world to the tangible reality around them. The ethereal outlines of the garden gradually crystallized into sharp focus as they returned to the present moment.

In synchrony, they took in slow, deliberate breaths, savoring the sensation of the air as it filled their lungs and then softly left their bodies. This act of mindfulness gradually reconnected them with their physical selves. They started to reawaken their limbs with subtle movements, wiggling fingers and toes, ensuring a gentle and unhurried revival from their deep meditative state.

As they completed this grounding ritual, their connection to the earth was re-established, and Amara and Chiyo slowly opened their eyes. With its dull colors and textures, the garden came back into complete clarity, welcoming them back to the tangible world.

Amara and Chiyo slowly stood up; the serenity from their meditation still lingered on their faces, manifesting in gentle smiles. They began walking back toward the house, but Amara abruptly paused. A subtle but distinct change in the atmosphere caught her heightened senses. Something felt amiss. It hung in the air between them, the way that an electric storm was detectable before it came.

Her meditative state had sharpened her perception, and as she glanced over her shoulder, sure enough, the silhouettes of five shadowy figures began emerging into her line of sight.

Equally perceptive of these approaching men, Chiyo turned to Amara, her eyes wide with apprehension and uncertainty.

"What should we do?" she asked, her voice shaking. "Should we get your mother from the house?"

"No," Amara responded firmly, swiftly unfastening the strap on her katana. Her voice carried a confidence tinged with eagerness. "We can handle this. chichi-ue has trained us for this, right?"

"But … But there are so many of them," Chiyo protested, her voice reflecting her worry, slightly fractured and stuttering. "But I see why Yasuke insisted we stay back … to protect Yuki."

Amara's eyes flashed with determination as she exchanged a meaningful glance with Chiyo.

"Then it's time we start protecting," she stated firmly. "Don't you think?" In the face of impending danger, her mind was especially set.

Drawing strength from Amara's composure, Chiyo nodded and mirrored Amara's actions, loosening the strap on her weapon.

They stood side by side, prepared to face the approaching threat, their training about to be tested in a way never experienced before.

As Tadashi and his men caught sight of Amara and Chiyo, a frown crept across their faces at the presence of the two young women standing their ground. However, undeterred, they quickened their pace, closing in on the girls. A profound silence enveloped the area, broken only by nature's subtle sounds.

"Can you hear them?" Amara whispered to Chiyo.

"Hear what?" Chiyo responded, her gaze on the approaching men.

"Their heartbeats. Listen as they draw nearer," Amara instructed, her senses sharply attuned to the enemies to this extent.

Chiyo refocused her attention on the men, channeling her energy toward sensing their presence. "Yes, I hear it now," she confirmed, her voice low. "They're nervous. Agitated. Unsure."

"Exactly!" Amara replied, excited.

She knew fear could be an advantage.

The men, now a mere twenty yards away, halted abruptly. "My name is Tadashi," one of them called out assertively. "I am Koichi's older brother."

"Who?" Amara asked nonchalantly, throwing a taunt into the mix.

Tadashi demanded, "Koichi, the man you killed. I am here for vengeance in his name. I plan to eradicate you and your family from this earth. Where are your parents?"

Inside the house, Yuki, alerted by the noise outside, approached the window. The sight of the men confronting Amara and Chiyo sent a chill through her. She quickly armed herself with her bow and arrows, moving stealthily toward the back door.

Yet she knew where to stop, not venturing into the fray yet.

Outside, Amara casually responded, "My parents are occupied. They have no part in this matter."

Tadashi sneered.

"Well, foolish, stubborn girl, I'll just leave their bodies beside yours. You can be a happy family together in death."

The air grew thick with anticipation as the men unsheathed their swords and readied their spears.

Tadashi started to swing his kusarigama menacingly.

Amara and Chiyo, katanas drawn, assumed their high guard stance. The moment was electric, charged with adrenaline and impending conflict. Tadashi signaled his men, and they charged with fierce focus, their sole intent to strike down the young women right there where they stood.

Amara's eyes narrowed as Tadashi charged, her body tensed for the imminent clash. But in a blur of motion, Yasuke appeared like a storm, positioning himself between his daughter and the oncoming threat. In a heartbeat, Tadashi was impaled by Yasuke's sword, Kurokaze. Tadashi's forward momentum had carried him onto the blade until the hilt graciously halted his advance.

The other assailants halted, appalled by this sudden turn of events. Kurokaze, now buried deep within Tadashi's abdomen, was gripped by a furious Yasuke. With a powerful yank, Yasuke not only withdrew the blade but also cleaved Tadashi's torso in two.

A rage unseen for years had ignited within Yasuke.

Amara and Chiyo, momentarily paralyzed by the sheer intensity of the moment, were jolted back to reality as one of Tadashi's men lunged at Yasuke. But before he could reach his target, an arrow whistled through the air, finding its mark in the assailant's skull.

They turned to see Yuki, bow poised, her expression a mask of indomitable ferocity.

Fueled by a battle cry, Amara redirected her focus to the remaining men. As one of them attacked in a blind rage, Amara deftly blocked the strike, though the force pushed her slightly off balance. Regaining her stance, she executed a precise kesa-giri, slashing diagonally, fatally wounding her adversary.

Chiyo, engaged in her own battle, narrowly dodged a lethal strike by rolling forward. As she prepared to retaliate, she caught sight of her opponent's head rolling past her, severed by Yasuke's swift intervention. With Kurokaze still dripping with blood, Yasuke extended a hand to help Chiyo up.

The final aggressor, driven by desperation, charged with his spear. But as he drew back to throw it, another of Yuki's arrows found its target, stopping him in his tracks.

His lifeless body crumpled to the ground, the threat extinguished.

The tension slowly ebbed away in the aftermath, leaving behind the stark reality of the fierce battle that had just unfolded.

Yasuke, Amara, Chiyo, and Yuki stood amidst the quiet that followed the storm, each processing the intensity and the swift brutality of the conflict that had ensued and ended so quickly.

Their eyes scanned the grim scene around.

Yasuke's heart, still racing from the fray, quickly turned to Amara and Chiyo, concern etched on his face.

"Is anyone injured?" he inquired urgently.

Amara and Chiyo exchanged a quick glance, assessing themselves for injuries.

"We're fine, I think," Amara finally answered, her voice steady despite the adrenaline still coursing hotly through her veins.

However, her voice bore a hint of relief.

A short distance away, Yuki, with the slightest nod, signaled that she was also unscathed. Her hand, still clutching her bow, was all the evidence needed to show her readiness to protect.

Amara, looking at the fallen adversaries, posed a practical question. "What should we do with these bodies? Do you think there will be more attackers?"

Yasuke, his gaze hardening as he considered the situation, replied, "No, I don't believe so. Hideyoshi is likely the only other person to know of these men's intentions, and I doubt he'll be causing us more trouble anytime soon."

Yasuke took a moment to collect his thoughts before issuing instructions. "Go inside, all of you, and clean yourselves up," he ordered, composed and masterful. "I will fetch the wagon and deal with the bodies of these men properly."

"I can help," Amara offered.

"No, I will return later this evening," Yasuke retorted. "Now go!"

In the wake of Yasuke's firm directive, Amara, Chiyo, and Yuki nodded in understanding, though still processing the intensity of the confrontation. Throughout the years, Yasuke had prepped them on the importance of swiftly managing the aftermath of such a violent encounter. It was both for their safety and to maintain the semblance of order in their home, a vital part of battle etiquette.

As the girls headed back to the house, Yasuke took a moment to follow them before veering off toward the stable to fetch the wagon. With a sense of urgency, he began the grim task of loading the remains of the fallen men.

His eyes frequently scanned the surroundings, acutely aware of the need for speed and caution in this delicate situation.

Once the bodies had been loaded, Yasuke collected the men's weapons, storing them in the stall before covering the wagon. He then steered the wagon deep into the dense forest, navigating through the thick foliage. As he journeyed deeper into the woods, the path grew increasingly secluded, and the light dimmer.

Yasuke crossed several isolated spots, each time contemplating whether to dispose of the bodies there. Yet, he had a particular location in mind, a place so remote that only those who had previously ventured there knew of its existence.

However, the location had been chosen for more than just its seclusion. The area was known to be a haunt for starving wild boars.

Yasuke reasoned that the boars, driven by hunger, would take care of the remains. This natural solution, though macabre, was a pragmatic way to ensure that no trace of the conflict would be found, allowing them to maintain a low profile.

Back at the house, the girls had finished cleansing themselves from the remnants of the conflict.

Visibly shaken by the day's events, Chiyo stood by the window, her gaze fixed on the site of the recent battle.

"That's a lot of blood," she remarked in a quiet voice, subdued as her eyes traced the bloodstained ground.

"It is. I'll fetch some buckets of water and wash it away," Amara proposed, her voice steady, placing a comforting hand on Chiyo's shoulder. "Nature will take care of the rest."

Amara felt a responsibility to maintain composure and manage the emotional climate of the household, especially given her prior experience with such confrontations.

Turning to Yuki, Amara inquired, "How are you faring, Okāsan?"

Yuki, her expression demonstrating relief and contemplation, responded, "I am fine, daughter. But what troubles me is your apparent calmness and lack of empathy for what's happened."

Yuki's voice carried more than a touch of consternation.

Amara met her mother's gaze, her expression indicating mild confusion. Yuki continued, "Yes, I had to end the lives of two men to protect our family, but I can't pretend it doesn't affect me, Amara."

In the silence that followed, punctuated only by the soft crackling of wood in the stove, Amara replied with a slight edge to her voice, "Why feel empathy for men who came with the intent to kill us?"

Her voice grew firmer, almost thunderous. "I cannot and will not show mercy to anyone who chooses to harm us. Please understand, Okāsan, this is not disrespect. However, I do not possess empathy for such individuals. That is the end of it. I would gladly cut down a hundred men without feeling if it meant ensuring our survival."

Yuki, seated and visibly unsettled by Amara's unwavering stance, nervously bounced her leg and fidgeted with her fingers.

Struggling to find the right words in response to Amara's declaration, she decided to steer their talk in a different direction.

"Very well, Amara," Yuki finally said, her voice striving for normalcy. "Could you and Chiyo help me prepare dinner?"

The shift in the conversation was Yuki's attempt to bring a sense of normalcy back to their household, or at least until Yasuke's return.

As the evening wore on, the atmosphere in the house was somber.

The routine task of preparing dinner unfolded in near silence, each family member absorbed in their thoughts, awaiting Yasuke's return. Their movements were mechanical, reflecting inner turmoil.

Chiyo moved about with a contemplative air.

The day's events had thrust her into a maelstrom of self-doubt. *Could I have taken a life if necessary?* she pondered, her thoughts circling the notion of what it truly meant to be a protector.

Yuki, meanwhile, was trapped in a psychological struggle, grappling with the stark reality of her actions. The fact of having taken lives, even in defense of her family, bore heavily on her.

She found herself caught between feelings of guilt and the necessity of survival. Yuki's internal battle was not just about reconciling her actions but also about reconciling her sense of self.

Is this who I am? she questioned silently, her thoughts spinning in confusion and introspection.

Amara's reflections had taken a different turn.

She contemplated a scenario in which Yasuke hadn't arrived in time. *Would Chiyo and I have been able to fend off the attackers on our own?*

The possibility of facing such danger without her father's intervention forced Amara to confront her capabilities and limitations. A slight anxiety started to rise inside her, feelings of being overshadowed by Yasuke's intervention revealing themselves as frustration. She channeled that frustration into sharpening her katana, the repetitive motion grounding her tumultuous thoughts.

"We could have been victorious," she mumbled to herself, the words consisting of both determination and lingering doubt.

CHAPTER TEN

From Ashes to Steel

(灰から鋼へ)

As dusk began to settle over the landscape, the distant sound of horse hooves and the rattle of a wagon broke the contemplative silence. These familiar sounds signaled Yasuke's return, providing a momentary break from the intense introspection gripping each of them. Their heads turned almost in unison toward the sound, apprehension and also relief in their eyes as they prepared to welcome Yasuke and discuss their next move.

The sounds of hearty eating filled the room during dinner, starkly contrasting the day's earlier tension. The slurping of soup from bowls resonated as each person, fatigued and famished from the day's ordeal, eagerly consumed their meal. There was an unspoken consensus not to bring up the fate of the attackers' remains.

The day's events had been so overwhelming that everyone silently agreed to move past it as if to leave the episode behind them.

After dinner, as Amara and Chiyo prepared for bed, Yuki and Yasuke settled in the quiet warmth of the fire. The silence lingered between them until Yuki ventured to break it.

"How are you holding up?" she asked gently.

"I'm managing, And you? How are you and the girls?" Yasuke replied, his voice carrying concern.

Yuki sighed, her gaze dropping. "It's devastating, naturally. But I understand the necessity of our actions. My brother instigated this whole situation. This could so easily have been avoided."

Her words were streaked with sorrow.

She paused, then continued with worry.

"Chiyo seems to be processing this the same way as me. But Amara, I'm concerned about her."

Yasuke listened as Yuki continued to voice her fears. "She seems emotionless, Yasuke. Unmoved, almost like a statue. And I fear that as she grows more powerful and skilled, she might lose her ability to feel for others. How do we help her find her heart again?"

Yasuke, understanding the gravity of Yuki's words, nodded. They had both observed the gradual change in Amara over the past year.

"I'll talk to her tonight," he stated.

Yuki looked up with relief.

"I think that would be best. She mustn't lose sight of her humanity amidst all this. She cannot be as cold as stone. She thinks it serves her, but it does not. Having no humanity in battle would render her as bad as any enemy we may face someday."

Yasuke said, "I agree. For me, making her a priority isn't just important, it's necessary. Perhaps my not pushing harder on these matters when she was younger added to this. I must make amends."

Yuki hesitated, turning to call Amara, then paused.

She glanced back at Yasuke.

"Shouldn't we wait until tomorrow? The girls just went to sleep."

"No more waiting," Yasuke replied. "The time for it is now."

Yuki continued her steps with a nod, informing Amara of Yasuke's request.

"Your father wants to speak with you," she said.

"Bring Chiyo as well!" Yasuke's voice echoed from the other room.

The girls, still awake, joined Yasuke around the fire.

The four of them sat in a circle, the atmosphere charged, all eyes on Yasuke.

"Listen, everyone," Yasuke started, his voice serious. "Being a warrior isn't just about swordsmanship, or even honor in the conventional sense. It's about understanding the gravity of life and death. Every time you draw your sword with the intent to kill, you alter not just your destiny but also the destinies of many others."

The fire's glow softly illuminated Yasuke's face as he prepared to reveal a deeply personal part of his history.

"Amara, when you were younger, I often went about, recounting tales of my battles and triumphs," he began, his voice resonant with so many untold memories. "Yet, there's a chapter of my early life, my true origin, that I've kept hidden until now. Judging from your mental path, Amara, it's time for you to know it."

As Yasuke's eyes lingered on the leaping flames, the present seemed to dissolve, allowing for the vivid recollection of his past.

The scene of his memory unfolded.

In the small, bustling coastal village of Mwamba, on the shores of Ilha de Moçambique, a young Yasuke was encountering experiences that would indelibly shape his destiny.

The scorching sun beat down on the arid East African coast, where the vast Indian Ocean relentlessly met the land.

Yasuke and his older brother, Chikondi, would spend long days at sea fishing for tuna and mackerel. Their catch was vital for their large family and the sustenance of their village. Everyone relied on it.

This region, including the mainland and the Ilha, fell under the powerful rule of the Kingdom of Monomotapa, which dominated southeastern Africa. The kingdom, known far and wide for its rich gold mines, had become a bustling hub of commerce and trade.

Its fame and wealth had not only reached the Portuguese but had also captivated them.

In their quest for exploration and trade along the East African coast, these people had become particularly interested in the resources and strategic position of the grand Monomotapa.

As Yasuke delved deeper into his story, the room seemed to resonate with the distant sounds of the ocean waves and the bustling life of Mwamba, transporting the girls and Yuki to the distant world of his childhood, a world that had laid the foundation for the man he had become, the one standing before them.

The Kingdom of Monomotapa had been renowned for its intricate social hierarchy, comprising diverse ethnic groups and tribes, each bringing its own unique customs and differing social structures.

This rich mixture of cultures added to the complexity of the kingdom's societal framework. Mwamba, Yasuke's village, had been integral to this elaborate social network.

The island's fertile soil and surrounding waters were a source of abundant agricultural produce and limitless fishing opportunities.

Yasuke's father, Zuberi, maintained the family through fishing, farming, and occasional gold mining. His monthly trips to the mainland to sell and trade their yields were expected among all of Mwamba's adult men. Even though gold was a rare find, their persistent trade efforts brought significant prosperity to the island.

As years passed and trade with Portugal intensified, the demand for agricultural products, gold, and fish surged. Aware of the island's bountiful resources, the kingdom began negotiating trade agreements with the village elders. Initially, the arrangement proved sustainable, but over time, the demand escalated, straining the delicate balance.

One evening, a pivotal discovery changed everything. The men of the island found gold, igniting a fiery gold rush within the village.

Many succeeded in unearthing the precious metal, subsequently trading it on the mainland. Their transactions, though discreet, eventually drew the attention of both the Kingdom of Monomotapa and the Portuguese traders, marking the beginning of a significant shift in the village's history and fate.

With the discovery of gold on the island, the king acted swiftly to control the island's ports and coastlines, preventing any interactions with foreign powers from now on.

All future trade with Mwamba and other villages was now to be funneled strictly through the king and his officials.

The once delicate negotiations with the village elders promptly dissolved, replaced by the kingdom's direct and oppressive control. The king's men regularly arrived on the island to mine for gold, excluding all the villagers of Mwamba and other inhabitants.

The elders from each tribe on the island convened a meeting to address this dire situation. The once idyllic Ilha de Moçambique had now lost much of its former splendor, its resources heavily exploited. The kingdom's initial pursuit of gold had expanded to overrunning agriculture and depleting the fishing grounds off the coast.

The villagers considered resistance, but they knew that facing the kingdom's advanced weaponry, acquired through trade with the Portuguese, would be tantamount to suicide. Firearms and other modern arms would decimate them swiftly.

Yasuke paused his story, his eyes brimming with tears in a rare display of vulnerability. The girls remained silent, absorbing the gravity of his words, providing him the space to compose himself.

As he resumed his tale, Yasuke brought them back to one fateful evening in Mwamba. The orange-golden sun had just started its descent toward the horizon. Yasuke and Chikondi were fishing near the coast when they noticed a massive, fortified vessel approaching.

Ships had grown common since the kingdom's arrival, but this one was different. Chikondi left for the village to investigate, urging Yasuke, "I think it's better if you stay behind."

Time passed. When Yasuke glanced back toward his homestead, he was astonished to see thick, dark smoke rising into the sky.

He quickly scrambled out of the water and headed back toward the village. As he moved away from the coast, a barrage of thunderous pops grew louder, and the smoke thickened. Panicked women and children, wounded and in pain, came running past.

Emerging from the smoke, he witnessed a horrific scene: men with firearms shooting at the villagers.

Having never encountered firearms, Yasuke realized these must be the source of the terrifying thunderous pops.

Yasuke's heart raced as he witnessed the horrific scene unfolding. Flames were consuming his village, the air soon filling with the screams of villagers and the crackle of burning homes.

Barefoot, he ran desperately through the chaos, the cold sand clinging to his feet. Fiery embers slowly danced from the sky as they started to burn Yasuke's skin. Frail huts made of wood and straw began collapsing around him, fueling the inferno.

Amidst the intensifying screams, Yasuke navigated through the turmoil, miraculously unharmed, determined to reach his home. The sight that met his eyes brought him to his knees in despair.

Before his home lay his two young brothers in a pool of blood, lifeless, mere children of five and eight years. Their tiny chests bore deep, fatal wounds. Only a few feet away, his mother lay gravely injured too, her body marked with vicious slashes that could only have come from a machete. She was still breathing, but her life was hanging by a thread. Yasuke rushed to her side, her blood-soaked, trembling hand caressing his cheek as tears streamed down his face.

In a faint whisper, he asked her, "Mother, what should I do?"

With a weak breath, she urged him, "Run, go find your father and older brother." She lay on the bloodied earth, gasping.

Startled by nearby gunfire, Yasuke turned to see his house collapse into ashes. When he looked back at his mother, she had taken her last breath, and he had missed it. Gently, he kissed her, then laid her head down on the ground and rose, his heart heavy with grief and shock.

Venturing through the remnants of his village, Yasuke stumbled upon two unfamiliar bodies, those of the assailants.

Pushing forward through the now clearing smoke, he then discovered the bodies of his brother, Chikondi, and father, Zuberi.

They had managed to take down two of the attackers, but it had cost them their lives. Time seemed to stop as Yasuke stood over them, his mind consumed by thoughts of anger and vengeance.

Wiping his eyes, he glanced back toward the continuing chaos, only to be spotted by two more assailants.

He turned and fled, weaving through the labyrinth of huts, using his intimate knowledge of the village's layout to evade his pursuers until he reached the island's opposite side. Now far from the gunfire and smoke, Yasuke found himself at the shoreline.

With the last of his strength, he pushed a small Ngalawa boat into the water and collapsed, lying flat on his back to catch his breath.

As the boat drifted away from the horror behind him, he sat up to look back one last time.

There, he saw other fortified vessels approaching the shore.

Despite the diligent efforts of the village elders, the kingdom's greed grew unchecked. Trade with the Portuguese had escalated, reaching a fever pitch. The recent shifts in political power were now demanding more resources than the mainland could ever supply.

The kingdom set its sights on the island in its insatiable quest for wealth. Their plan was simple yet ruthless: to take complete control of the island and all of its resources. The small community, barely numbering over a hundred adults and around a hundred and sixty children, stood little chance against the kingdom's might.

The kingdom had deemed the inevitable bloodshed an acceptable sacrifice for the lucrative rewards of trade with the Portuguese and other international powers. The villagers' lives and the safety of the children had been mere pawns in their grand scheme of commerce and power. The assailants had never known what empathy meant.

As Yasuke's tiny boat drifted farther into the open waters, the cacophony of destruction on the island faded into the distance.

Now just a sliver above the horizon, the sun was only managing to cast a dimming light over the sea. Yasuke, with a fierce intensity in his stare, looked back at the only place he had ever called home.

The harrowing sight of palm trees engulfed in flames and huts crumbling to ashes was mirrored in his eyes, reflecting devastation.

The realization that his entire way of life had been irreversibly altered and that his friends and family had been mercilessly sacrificed for mere resources fueled a growing sense of vengeance and hatred in him. In that solemn moment, as the darkness of night began to envelop the sky, Yasuke's path seemed to narrow.

It was becoming one driven by a singular purpose: revenge.

Three days had passed by the time Yasuke's boat, battered by relentless tides and a searing sun, finally reached a distant shore.

Exhausted, famished, and consumed by his burning desire for vengeance, he staggered onto the land.

Too weak and sick to continue, Yasuke began to dry heave, struggling to catch his breath. His eyes bulged, his vision was blurry, and his dehydrated, salted body was crying out for water.

Yet he noticed an indistinct silhouette approaching.

Before he could discern the figure, he collapsed, unconscious.

A middle-aged fisherman, out gathering his daily catch, discovered Yasuke. Unbeknownst to Yasuke, this place would soon become a haven. The fisherman and family who took him in vehemently opposed the kingdom of Monomotapa's years of ruthless atrocities.

News of the kingdom's recent brutal deeds had traveled swiftly, and this family had stood firmly against such perceived inhumanity.

When Yasuke awoke, therefore, it was not to see a weapon being wielded at his head, nor to hear words of aggression coming his way.

Instead, he was greeted with fresh water and fish, and with caring smiles and words that urged him to eat and drink, regaining strength.

He warmed to the family immediately, sharing the ordeal of his village. His voice quivered with barely restrained rage.

He recounted the horrors he had witnessed, his declaration to seek revenge echoing with conviction.

His youthful visage, once innocent, now bore the steely eyes of one determined to avenge his lost kin and compatriots.

The family, deeply moved by his tale and his unshakeable willpower, vowed to support him, seeing in him not just a young man engulfed in sorrow and fury, but a fine warrior in the making.

Under their guidance, Yasuke began a rigorous training program. The man and his eldest son had both served in the kingdom's military and possessed extensive knowledge of the eternal workings of war.

Their military knowledge shaped his innate abilities and instructed him on the subtleties of warfare. With each passing day, he refined his swordsmanship, learned battle strategies, and trained his body to withstand severe conditions. His skills became sharper, and his mission clearer. Yasuke was intent on gaining entry into the kingdom's military academy, where he could strike at the core of its military power and deliver his just revenge.

As years passed, Yasuke's transformation was profound. Once a young, peaceful fisherman, he had now become an imposing warrior, but his evolution had not been without its struggles. He wrestled with the depth of his sorrow, the intensity of his vengeful desires, and the fear of losing his essence to his dark quest. Yet, his will to confront the kingdom that had ravaged his life remained unshaken.

After six and a half years, now a young man of seventeen, Yasuke felt ready to pursue the vengeance for which he had so long yearned.

Not a day or night had passed without thoughts of retribution.

His adoptive family, understanding and nurturing his quest, had also used their well-honed military connections to secure Yasuke a position as a guard within the kingdom's army.

Yasuke's soul turned into a chasm in the army, tormented by unending visions of retribution. In the quietness of the early morning hours, he revisited in his mind the devastation of his village, each replay ending with a more brutal outcome for the culprits.

He meticulously studied the military base's routines, noting every detail about the soldiers' movements, meals, and habits.

Each day, Yasuke's eyes, burning with intensity, meticulously scanned the Royal Court, observing its high-ranking chiefs and seasoned warriors, the very men who might have been the instruments of the king's lethal commands. The memory of his family and villagers, unjustly torn from this world, was stoking a fire within him that not even the deepest rivers could quench.

The path to the king was fraught with peril, a complex journey that could claim his life at any turn. Yet, Yasuke was determined, driven by a singular purpose eclipsing all fear. To confront the king was to stare into the abyss of his own haunted soul, but Yasuke was firm in facing this ultimate challenge, ready to sacrifice everything to avenge the ghosts haunting his every step.

On the seventh anniversary of the harrowing day that had forever altered his life, Yasuke chose the cover of night to enact his long-awaited retribution. He knew it was impossible to accomplish his mission in a single night; it had to be a methodical process, eliminating guards one by one under the veil of darkness.

Nightfall provided Yasuke the advantage of stealth and secrecy, not least essential for disposing of the bodies without raising alarm.

He was acutely aware that if any of the soldiers went absent from training, they would likely be presumed deserters, a common occurrence in the kingdom's army. This knowledge was crucial to his plan, allowing him to remove carefully and strategically those in his path, bringing him closer to his ultimate target each successive night.

As darkness enveloped the military grounds, Yasuke, cloaked in shadows, moved with lethal precision.

The subdued sounds of a muffled and quickly ended struggle intermittently pierced the still night air, stifled as Yasuke methodically eliminated two more guards, though not of the desired high rank.

Over the years, Yasuke had often pondered how he would feel when he finally embarked on his long-anticipated journey of revenge.

For the moment he executed the first guard, a chilling sensation coursed through him. Goosebumps erupted on his skin, swiftly followed by a searing heat as his blade, previously unstained, found its mark, slicing cleanly through the man's spine.

A sense of complete empowerment and euphoria overwhelmed him; he realized that his long-awaited retribution had begun, flooding his being with an intense, almost intoxicating feeling.

Yasuke's preparations for this moment had been meticulous, not just mentally but physically as well.

At a mere seventeen years of age, his imposing stature had already surpassed that of many fully grown men, lending him a physical advantage that made his first kill less challenging than anticipated.

The soldier never saw it coming as he had been ambushed while returning from relieving himself.

Yasuke then set his sights on the second guard with a ruthless determination devoid of empathy. The ensuing physical struggle ended with Yasuke overpowering and strangling his opponent.

In these moments, he realized a grim truth: he could execute a thousand men and his relentless quest for revenge would always overshadow any vestiges of empathy for those he had eliminated.

He became consumed with planning his next moves, pushing aside any lingering emotions to focus solely on his objective.

Yasuke, with a calculated coldness, meticulously planned each act, ensuring he remained undetected until he could fulfill his ultimate mission of assassinating the king. He deliberately paced his retribution, targeting one or two soldiers each week. As time progressed, each act of violence grew more gruesome than the last.

Night after night, the silent shadows of the military compound became his domain. With each soldier he eliminated, Yasuke was moving closer to the king, the architect of his people's suffering. Yet, with each life taken, a part of Yasuke's humanity was ebbing away, replaced by an unyielding resolve hardened by the memories of his lost home and the cries of those who could no longer speak out.

Over two months, Yasuke had stealthily assassinated fifteen soldiers, yet none of these had held high ranks. Strangulation had become his common method, but increasingly, he was finding a grim satisfaction in the lethal elegance of his blade. As his frustration mounted, so did Yasuke realize the need to adjust his strategy.

Tension began to rise within the ranks of the soldiers too.

Whispers were turning into murmurs of concern as they noticed the growing number of their comrades failing to return their posts, especially at night. The unsettling pattern sparked unease and suspicion among them, prompting discussions laced with confusion.

"Why are so many not returning?" they queried among themselves with apprehension. "Where do they go to, after darkness falls?"

"And they are some of our most loyal and capable men," some would say, bemused and perplexed about their missing men.

The absence of so many, once attributed to desertion, now seemed too frequent and too similarly timed to be mere coincidence. Besides, as some were pointing out, a few of the missing were those who had shunned the very thought of desertion, finding it abhorrent.

Some guardians of the king's chamber began speculating that the missing soldiers might be escaping aboard Portuguese trade ships.

This theory sparked additional concern, leading to heightened awareness. The king's chief protector made a decisive move.

He would address these growing uncertainties by temporarily ceasing all trade activities and commanding that all foreign ships depart from their land by the month's end. They had to be gone.

Yasuke, aware of these rising suspicions, knew he had to act swiftly. Each passing day brought an increased risk of his imminent discovery, and he could not afford to be exposed before reaching his ultimate target. He began to plan more daring, high-profile assassinations, targeting those in positions of power within the ranks.

The stakes were higher, but so were the potential rewards.

In the still of one particular night, Yasuke moved silently through the military compound. This night would bring the opportunity he had been waiting for. It was not long until he spotted two high-ranking military officers standing guard outside the king's quarters.

These elite guards, vigilant and imposing, presented a most formidable barrier to the inner sanctum in which the king rested.

As the hours wore on and the temperature dipped, the only sound breaking the silence was the occasional cough from soldiers in the nearby barracks. Yasuke, solid in his vigil, observed the elite guards intently. He understood their skill level was unmatched in the army, making a surprise attack by far his best strategy.

His moment arrived when a palace guard approached to relieve one of the elites. Yasuke seized this chance, stealthily following the departing guard outside the bounds of their secure compound.

He maintained a safe distance as the guard ventured toward some bushes, presumably for a brief respite.

Like a predator homing in on its target, Yasuke silently unsheathed his blade. His eyes, sharp and focused, followed the guard's every move. He crept closer, stealthy, poised for the kill.

As the guard sensed a presence and turned around, it was too late.

Yasuke, his blade gripped tightly in both hands, leaped forward, his silhouette framed against the moonlit sky, descending upon the unsuspecting guard. With a swift, brutal force, Yasuke struck the guard multiple times in the chest, his actions quick and lethal.

The guard collapsed without a sound, crumpling.

Drenched in blood, Yasuke struggled to maintain his grip as he dragged the guard's body deeper into the thicket of bushes, intending to hide it temporarily before moving it to his regular disposal site.

Back at the king's quarters, tensions were mounting.

The remaining elite guard, accompanied by a younger palace guard, was growing increasingly agitated. The seasoned warrior's face showed signs of stress as he scanned the surroundings, evidently troubled by his partner's prolonged absence. The man had been relieved of his duties, so his time was his own, but this was not usual.

It also was not protocol; everyone knew that an absence would spark fractious unrest in the compound. It could signify a stealth attack.

"Where did he go? I thought he would have been back by now," he said, slightly irritated. The longer any guard was missing, the more the others needed to fret about him instead of attending to their duties. "Stay put here," the elite guard said to the junior guard.

He set off, intent on searching for his missing comrade.

Yasuke, anticipating this move, had concealed himself behind a large wagon loaded with barrels. Peering out from his hiding spot, he noticed the guard's heightened alertness; the man unsheathed his sword almost immediately upon descending the stairs. Yasuke's heart pounded in his chest as he assessed the situation. The guard was physically imposing and skilled, presenting a formidable challenge.

The tension within Yasuke escalated to near breaking point as he readied himself to strike. However, his plan was abruptly halted.

Six soldiers unexpectedly appeared, strolling across the courtyard.

The elite guard swiftly approached them, inquiring about his partner. Their responses offered no clues, but they did deter Yasuke.

At least, they foiled his easy plan to take out the elite guard.

Yasuke, though mentally primed for the attack, recognized the disadvantage of his position against the odds. He decided against action, realizing the risk of confronting such a number was too great.

Instead, Yasuke mentally retreated for now, waiting in the shadows, his every sense attuned to the perfect moment to strike. However, as the night waned and the first light of dawn approached, his opportunity had slipped away. With a heavy heart, he retreated to the barracks, kicking at the ground, his face full of disappointment.

Exhausted from the night's vigil, Yasuke dressed sluggishly, steeling himself for the day's training. His routine was unexpectedly interrupted when a guard called him to the Royal Court.

A surge of apprehension swept over him. *Have they discovered my secret? Is this the end for me?* he wondered anxiously.

To his utter astonishment, events took a far more positive course; by order of the Royal Court, he had been promoted to the position of an elite guard, replacing the now-presumed deserter.

Yasuke's extraordinary physical strength and combat abilities had also not been overlooked during training. His skill in warding off multiple assailants had drawn the gaze of the king's chief protector.

Despite his tender age, there was a conviction that Yasuke possessed the potential to evolve into an extraordinary warrior.

This twist of fate was the opening Yasuke had been desperately seeking, sending a rush of exhilaration surging through him.

Now, he would be in a prime position to carry out his mission.

He accepted the role without hesitation, suppressing both empathy and remorse for his past actions.

Following his appointment, Yasuke was transferred to a different set of barracks, the dwelling of the elite and high-ranking guards.

Now, he could put a different plan into action, one he was still nurturing. He intended to patiently observe for a few weeks to familiarize himself with the routines, also sharpening his skills by training with more seasoned guards than he had been used to.

After one week, Yasuke's new role as an elite guard was providing him with unprecedented access and knowledge. He was quickly learning the compound's most closely guarded secrets, including access to discreet discussions, hidden doors, and concealed walls.

His training allowed him to navigate the king's main chamber with increased stealth and silence, even discovering a secret escape route within the king's sleeping quarters. Assigned to stand guard overnight outside the king's quarters twice a week, Yasuke perceived this to be the perfect opportunity. Now, he could exact long-awaited revenge.

Yet, as he edged closer to his goal, Yasuke's mind became a tumultuous hive of conflicting thoughts and emotions. He found himself grappling with a relentless internal struggle between the desire for escape and the possibility of capture.

For years, his soul had been consumed by anger and the meticulous planning of an act of revenge.

He had even come to terms with the likelihood of being captured in his quest for vengeance.

But now, as the moment of action approached, a new consideration emerged, challenging him: it was a fresh thought, the prospect of a life beyond this singular vengeful pursuit.

The following day, Yasuke found himself still lost in a maelstrom of thoughts, pacing the compound grounds like a vulture in an erratic orbit around its prey. His mind, deeply entangled in contemplation, was barely registering his surroundings. His restless wandering, however, was abruptly halted. He strained to listen, overhearing a conversation in another tongue.

It came from the other side of the wall.

The words he caught sent his heart pounding like the resonant beats of drums at an East African celebration.

It was the Portuguese, and in compliance with the chief protector's recent edict, they were discussing their imminent departure from Africa, set to occur before the break of dawn.

This revelation presented Yasuke with a sudden, unanticipated chance to escape. Yet, he realized with a sinking heart that he was far from ready, neither mentally nor physically.

The last few days had seen him so engulfed in his entangled turbulent thoughts that he hadn't prepared for such an opportunity.

Moreover, even if he succeeded in assassinating the king, he would have to face the chief protector, a physically imposing figure and highly skilled in combat. Yasuke understood that an encounter with him would likely lead to his death. This was not in his plan.

As the day unfolded, the sun's strong rays seared the arid, parched landscape of the East African compound. Despite the overwhelming heat, the trees were swaying gently in the hot breeze, their movement a stark contrast to the stillness of the surroundings.

Yasuke lay in wait inside the barracks, his upcoming night shift looming. The oppressive heat seemed only to magnify his anxiety and restlessness, each moment stretching interminably.

Then, in an unexpected shift, his anxiety began ebbing away, much like the receding waters after a high tide's crash against the shore.

His mind began wandering into the realm of faded memories, each recollection a vivid echo of his past. He saw again the lifeless bodies of his brothers lying in the dust, a scene from that devastating day seven years ago. The memory of his mother's last breath in his arms cast an impassive, almost emotionless mask over his face.

The distant echoes of Mwamba, his lost home, resonated in his mind as he closed his eyes, succumbing to deep, dark slumber.

Hours later, Yasuke awoke as if transformed. It was as if the melding of his past and the intensity of his determination had forged something new within him—a turning point in his very essence.

As the sun dipped toward the horizon, marking the end of another day, Yasuke began preparing for his guard duty. He moved with a renewed sense of purpose, his actions deliberate and focused. The evening's shadows cloaked the compound, and in this twilight, Yasuke stepped out, ready to face whatever this night would bring.

Dressed in his guard uniform, Yasuke moved with confidence and authority, his broad shoulders shifting rhythmically with each purposeful stride. The compound was unusually lively and vibrant that night, buzzing with the sounds of soldiers helping the Portuguese with their many final preparations for departure.

Amidst all the hustle, some soldiers were even selling or trading personal items, a last-minute attempt to generate wealth.

Yasuke noticed the chief protector's conspicuous absence as he ascended the stairs to relieve the current guard on duty. This absence was significant; it indicated that the king was not in his quarters.

Over the past few weeks of observation, Yasuke had noted that the chief protector would only leave the king's side twice each night, a pattern that might well play out to Yasuke's advantage.

Despite the cover of night, the air within the palace compound remained hot and heavy, oppressive, and adding a palpable intensity to the atmosphere. Stationed at their post, Yasuke and the other guard could hear the distinct sound of footsteps approaching.

The king was returning to his quarters now, flanked by the chief protector and a contingent of guards. The king and his entourage passed by Yasuke and his fellow guard without a glance.

The chief protector entered the king's quarters first, conducting a thorough search to ensure the area remained secure.

Once he signaled the all-clear, the king proceeded inside, with the chief protector following closely behind and shutting the door.

Yasuke, standing watch outside, felt a surge of adrenaline. This was the moment he had been waiting for, the culmination of his long-held plans for vengeance. Now, with the king so close, the reality of his mission and the gravity of what he was about to attempt weighed heavily upon him.

The earlier commotion within the compound subsided, leaving a tense silence. Yasuke, stationed at his post for hours, took advantage of the lull to use the latrine area outside the compound. He informed the guards below, ensuring a temporary replacement for his duty.

His return was swift, aiming to miss no chance should the chief protector lower his guard. Surprisingly, during his brief absence, he crossed paths with the chief protector himself.

The man was also heading toward the latrines.

Realizing the moment's opportunity, Yasuke hastened back to his post, where he discreetly relieved the stand-in guard. With the king presumed alone and vulnerable in his chamber, Yasuke decided that the time to act was now. Standing guard, he allowed himself a few seconds of contemplation, which stretched into what felt like an eternity. Then, with the swiftness of a hot wind brushing against his face, he unsheathed his short blade. Without so much as a glance, he attacked the accompanying guard with a swift, decisive strike to the throat, his actions as forceful as waves assaulting the shore. He caught the guard's body, preventing any sound that might alert others.

After peeking around the corridor to ensure the other soldiers had not been alerted, Yasuke faced the unexpected obstacle of a locked door. Of course … The chief protector had taken the precaution of securing the king's quarters before his departure.

Beads of sweat formed on Yasuke's brow. He worked to pick the lock, stealing constant glances over the balcony to ensure he remained undetected. The tension and silence were deafening.

But at last, the lock yielded with a defining click, marking the irreversible step into his carefully planned destiny.

Yasuke entered the dimly lit room, where a single candle was creating elongated shadows across the chamber. Approaching the king's bed, he observed the rhythmic rise and fall of the monarch's chest. Yet, the presence of death loomed large, slowly awakening the ruler. At initial glance, he would have assumed the figure was the chief protector—until the word "Mwamba" was whispered by Yasuke. His eyes widened, and before he could get out a scream, the young warrior's blade was already plunging deep into his chest.

In the candle's dim light, Yasuke became an instrument of his own pent-up wrath, delivering strike after merciless strike.

It was a tempest of steel and blood, until the count of his blows became lost in the fervor of his long-awaited act.

Collecting himself after the furious assault, Yasuke eyed the secret escape route but paused to enact one final act of defiance.

He wiped his blood-soaked hands and blade on the sheets. Then, taking the candle, he set the bed and blankets on fire, fanning the flames to ensure they began consuming the room.

With the fire set, he escaped through the secret door, leaving behind the chaos of his retribution and stepping into the unknown.

Yasuke navigated the dark, constricted stairway, his steps unsteady as the distant sounds of commotion echoed through the walls.

He dropped his blade in his rush, but the enveloping darkness made it impossible to find again. Pushing forward regardless, he glimpsed a sliver of light seeping through a narrow crevice leading to a door. The entry was so small he had to crawl to get through, and he soon realized he was moving through an underground tunnel.

After what felt like an eternity, he emerged from the ground at the compound's rear.

As he gasped for air, Yasuke noticed the Portuguese ships preparing to set sail, their ropes being pulled in.

This offered his opportunity.

He bolted toward the boat, now inching away from the dock. Drawing upon the swimming skills honed in his youth, Yasuke threw himself into the ocean, battling the waves with powerful strokes.

He had grown up as a skilled swimmer, this expertise now aiding his desperate escape. With a final burst of energy, he clambered onto the ship, grasping the last rope that trailed in the water.

On board, Portuguese sailors glanced back in shock and confusion, witnessing the huge flames that had begun to engulf parts of the royal compound. A flurry of panicked shouts filled the ship as it steadily moved from the shore.

Passing unnoticed amidst so much noise and chaos, Yasuke quickly concealed himself in the ship's food storage, hiding behind sacks of grain and rice. He became a stowaway, hidden in shadows.

As the first light of dawn pierced through the swiftly moving clouds, the chief protector, accompanied by members of the royal army, began thoroughly examining the blaze's horrific aftermath.

The fire had consumed nearly three-quarters of the compound, leaving once majestic pillars and columns nothing but charred husks.

The chief protector, suspecting foul play in the fire's origins, was attempting to piece together the previous night's events.

The king's chambers remained inaccessible from the main entrance, still radiating heat and partially smoldering.

He could only surmise the king might still be safe in his quarters, but he could not know—yet. The entrance was burned, but at the other side, perhaps His Highness' heavy door had stopped the fire.

Opting for an alternative route, he ventured through the escape tunnel at the back, intent on swiftly reaching the king's bedchamber.

Guided by the dim light of day filtering through, he navigated the tunnel and ascended the stairs, the air growing warmer as he approached. In the dark stairwell, he stumbled upon something odd—a short knife, the kind commonly carried by elite soldiers.

Initial confusion quickly gave way to anger, the evidence suggesting a sinister plot that had not hitherto entered his mind.

Entering through the remnants of a once sturdy door now eaten away by flames, he was confronted with the harrowing sight of the king's charred bones amid the ashes of the wooden bed frame.

The discovery of the knife only deepened his conviction that a soldier had to be behind this heinous act. Exiting through the back, he sprinted shoreward. The Portuguese vessel had long since vanished, having set sail hours earlier.

He took a pause by the water's edge, a brief sojourn there to consider everything and attempt to piece it together.

The tide is unusually low, he noted.

However, nothing could prepare him for what his eyes saw next.

A grim survey along the shoreline unveiled a sight more appalling than the fire's aftermath: the lifeless bodies of over fifteen soldiers, their features bloated and unrecognizable, bound and anchored to boulders meant to keep them submerged in the shallow cove's waters.

Overwhelmed by a torrent of rage, the chief protector stood immobilized, his gaze fixed on the hideous watery grave.

The enormity of the betrayal before him ignited a fury as potent as one thousand burning suns, rendering him momentarily powerless as he contemplated the magnitude of the betrayal.

Which one of our soldiers could be capable of such an atrocity?

Amara coughed, breaking the tableau, and the dark room came back into view. The group, wrapped in the intensity of Yasuke's tale, hadn't even realized the fire had died.

Eager for more, Amara pressed, "So, then what happened, Chichi-ue?"

Yasuke, usually calm and composed, paused.

There was a distant look in his eyes, reflecting a sorrow rarely shown. The unveiling of a tale buried in his memory for over thirty years made him appear unusually vulnerable, as if the memories were meant to remain as undisturbed as a sealed and inaccessible tomb.

After a moment of heavy silence, Yasuke cleared his throat.

His voice, initially, was trembling.

"What happened next? Well, I was discovered three days later. The Portuguese wanted to throw me overboard; they were not aware of my deeds at the compound, but they were unwilling to harbor a stowaway, no matter what."

He paused, gathering his thoughts.

Yuki rekindled the fire, sending shadows across the room.

"To them, I was just a useless young black boy, barely understanding their language and not remotely useful to them. The captain eventually made me work on menial tasks aboard the vessel, essentially enslaving me. I toiled under their command for three whole years, performing the grueling tasks of a deckhand and ship's cook. Among other duties. But I shall not bore you with everything."

Yuki interrupted, "Why didn't you flee at one of the ports?"

"To where?" Yasuke countered. "Where could I have fled to?"

"Anywhere but there!" Amara's voice reflected her frustration. It was a disappointment to hear of her capable father rendered so weak.

Yasuke, now with a steadier voice, responded, "Other lands were no sanctuary for someone of my skin, dear daughter. For all their faults, the Portuguese were the devils I knew. In that first year, my heart was filled with anger, and I often thought of slaying the men on the ship for their mistreatment. But over time, I made friends, allowing reflection to replace my rage. Besides, it was clear I could not go around killing everyone with whom I disagreed in life."

He laughed faintly. The quip was not appreciated; his daughter's face remained stern and filled with anguish over the tale. Her expression seemed to say, 'but why? Why could you not kill them?'

Grasping Amara's hand, he continued, "Amara, I realized that my relentless pursuit of vengeance, the endless cycle of violence, had brought neither my family back nor had it filled the void in my soul. It had not made me happy. But as for the king … he met the fate he deserved. At least I had this small solace."

Yasuke was confidently nodding his head.

He went on, "But the soldiers, especially the young, innocent ones I killed on my path to the king, they were not to blame for Mwamba."

Yasuke's voice carried so much regret.

"Those are lives I wrongfully took, and those are the heavy and heartfelt burdens I will carry with me to hell. Empathy for them grew within me over time, you see? You, Amara, must find balance too.

"Yes, a samurai must protect and uphold family and honor. War necessitates action, but indiscriminate killing, on the other hand, can only ever serve to poison the soul. We must aim our wrath only at those who warrant it, finding strength in restraint and wisdom in our battles. This is the essence of our way, the path of the samurai."

Yasuke scanned the room, noting the expressions of those around him. Yuki's face was a portrait of serene sadness mixed with relief.

At the same time, Chiyo's impassive expression barely concealed the emotional turmoil in her eyes, like a dam holding back a relentless surge. But it was Amara's reaction that Yasuke had been anticipating.

After a moment of silence, a stark transformation occurred.

Amara's face softened, illuminated by a dawning understanding, her lips curving into a gentle smile as she rose to her feet.

Yasuke, feeling the burden of hours spent in reflection, stood alongside her, his towering presence meeting her stare.

"Chichi-ue ... umm ... Sensai!" Amara's voice, filled with newfound clarity and tremors of realization, broke the silence.

"I now see the world through your mind. Your wisdom has opened my eyes. Chichi-ue, you are saying that my rage was consuming me, a shadow darkening my spirit during meditation."

As tears began to well, Amara attempted to brush them away, a futile effort to contain such an overwhelming emotion.

Yasuke's face softened into an expression of genuine happiness. Amara's use of 'sensai,' a term she hadn't uttered in years, signaled to him a readiness to embrace his teachings once more.

"I have much left to teach you, all of you!" Yasuke affirmed.

"We are ready to receive your wisdom," Amara replied, her conviction rallying Chiyo and Yuki to her side.

The day's battle and the night's heavy discussions had started taking its toll on them all.

"Let's rest now," Yasuke suggested, acknowledging the need to recover physically and emotionally. "Tomorrow, we realign our mastery over our ki and seishin, our spiritual energy." With that, the girls retreated to their quarters, the urgency of their steps echoing their eagerness for guidance.

Yasuke lingered by the dimming fire, lost in thought as dawn began to edge the sky with light.

Yuki approached, her voice soft but insistent. "Come," she urged, a knowing smile on her lips. "Even the great Yasuke needs his rest."

Yasuke allowed himself a moment more by the fire before finally yielding to Yuki's wisdom.

CHAPTER ELEVEN

Perennial Spirits

(多年生の精霊)

Weeks had passed since Yasuke had unveiled the haunting saga of his past, a rare glimpse into his vulnerabilities. Yet, the fortress of his stoicism had been quickly rebuilt, leaving no trace of weakness.

In the household, a newfound equilibrium had emerged as the training and meditation sessions with the girls gained deeper significance, influenced profoundly by Yasuke's revelations.

It was evident that his words had pierced the previously impenetrable void in Amara's soul, seeding a transformative change.

The season was shifting now, with the air warmer than usual for the time of year, signaling an early arrival of spring.

Yasuke predicted the crops and flowers would awaken from their winter slumber sooner, prompting him to plan a visit to Midoriya.

His intentions were threefold: to gather supplies for Yuki's garden and the hens he had recently begun to breed; and to gauge the current sentiment of the settlement, especially after his last encounter marred by the uncomfortable stares drawn by the now slain Tadashi's recruitment efforts. More so, the third of his intentions, he needed to confirm that Hideyoshi had not made an unwelcome return.

Meanwhile, outside of the house, the air was electric with the thunderous claps of wooden bokkens clashing, each strike speaking for the reawakened intensity of Amara and Chiyo's training sessions. In a sudden twist, Amara halted the combat, skillfully blocking Chiyo's final strike with her bokken. A silent signal passed between them as their focus was abruptly drawn to Yasuke approaching the stall, evidently preparing the horse for a journey.

With a shared look of surprise and curiosity that was almost obvious, Amara and Chiyo's exchanged glance spoke volumes. Without uttering a word, they sprinted toward Yasuke, propelled by anticipation and the unexpected thrill of the unknown.

"Are you headed to Midoriya?" Amara demanded to know, her voice holding a note of suspense.

Yasuke, absorbed in his task with the horse, did not answer.

"May Chiyo and I accompany you?" she persisted, her voice betraying her desperate need for his acknowledgment.

Yasuke finally spoke as he guided the horse from the stall.

"Why do you wish to go?" he asked.

Amara hurried to explain. "Chichi-ue … after everything that's occurred recently, we could use a change of scenery."

Yasuke offered no verbal acknowledgment of Amara's reasoning. Yet, internally, he found himself in agreement. The girls had been trapped in the aftermath of a recent brutal event, forced to witness lingering traces of conflict without a brief moment's relief to cleanse their thoughts. Sweeping a glance toward the field, the site of the recent bloodshed, Yasuke noted the dark stains that defaced the earth, grim witness to the turmoil they had all endured.

Without uttering a word, he acknowledged Amara's request in his own way, starting to clear space in the wagon for Amara and Chiyo.

The wagon jostled along the familiar path, the consistent clip-clop of hooves punctuating the travelers' heavy anticipation.

Amara's eyes sparkled with a youthful fervor not seen in ages, a fleeting glimpse of the girl she once had been.

Chiyo, too, seemed lighter, the onerous nature of their recent trials momentarily lifted from her shoulders as she leaned into Amara's embrace. As they approached the lively marketplace of Midoriya, the vibrant colors and bustling activity promised a welcome distraction from the many dark shadows lingering back at home.

Yet, for Yasuke, the journey held a different purpose.

His eyes were steadfast, fixated on the direction of Hideyoshi's stall. He scrutinized the surroundings with each step closer to the center, seeking any sign of the man who had caused the disruption to their peace. Finding the booth deserted, Yasuke's focus shifted.

Now, it fell on the task at hand.

Though attracting the usual curious glances due to their noticeably dark skin, nothing overtly suspicious seemed to come from the crowd. Leaving the girls to explore the marketplace, Yasuke tended to his errands. Meanwhile, Amara and Chiyo wandered among the stalls, their laughter mingling with the chatter of merchants and patrons.

Yet amidst the hustle and bustle, their attention was drawn to a poignant sight, that of several young girls, destitute and alone.

It was a scene Amara had witnessed before, striking a chord deep within Chiyo, stirring memories of her own past abandonment.

Sensing the turmoil within Chiyo, Amara gently took her hand, offering silent support. "Do you think—?"

"Yes," Chiyo interjected, her response swift, carrying certainty. "Yes, they've been abandoned, just like I was."

Chiyo's words echoed a bitter truth, acknowledged with a somber nod by Amara.

"It seems our fathers were indeed wise to the ways of the world," Chiyo murmured.

With a firm grasp, Amara led Chiyo toward one of the girls, a figure who stood out amidst the hustle of the marketplace.

Clad in a tattered white shirt and worn pants, the girl's tall, slender frame belied her youth, though her eyes, wide with apprehension, betrayed a vulnerability drawing both Amara and Chiyo to her side.

"Who are you?" Amara inquired with curiosity and empathy, reaching out to bridge the gap.

"I am Sakura," the young girl replied, her voice barely above a whisper.

"Like the cherry blossom tree?" Chiyo asked with enthusiasm.

"Yes … just like the tree," Sakura replied.

"I'm Amara, and this is Chiyo, my sister in spirit. Why are you here by yourself, looking so deserted?"

Sakura's eyes darted around, her body tensing as if preparing to flee from some unseen danger.

"What … what … what do you mean? I'm not alone. I'm waiting for my mother," she stammered, her voice quivering.

The hollowness in her assertion was obvious to Amara and Chiyo.

They shared a knowing glance, recognizing the facade of bravery in Sakura's denial.

They stood in silent solidarity, deciding their next move.

"We're here to help," Chiyo said gently. "Not long ago, I found myself in your same situation, roaming this marketplace, forsaken by my own family over a debt they couldn't pay."

Sakura remained silent, her eyes fixed on the ground as if acknowledging their kindness would shatter her fragile veneer of hope. The bustling sounds of the marketplace enveloped them, a stark contrast to the quiet despair hanging between the trio.

"No. You do not understand. I am waiting for my mother," Sakura repeated, more to herself than to Amara and Chiyo.

Her eyes drifted to the distance, her voice fading into a tremble, leaving an echo of her longing captured in the air.

Sakura began walking in the opposite direction, but Amara's piercing call halted her retreat. "Your mother is not coming, Sakura!"

Amara said it with urgency and compassion, reaching out to the retreating figure. Sakura paused, her back still to them, the silence burdened by unspoken truths. The air felt leaden.

"I know … I know," Sakura whispered back with acceptance and yet still with resistance. The admission was a hard-fought battle within herself, each word a step toward facing her reality.

"Where are you from?" Amara pressed gently, seeking to understand more of Sakura's story.

With a slow, reluctant turn, Sakura faced them again, her eyes glossy with the sheen of unshed tears.

"Asagiri was … is my home. It's a place wrapped in beauty, where misty mornings greet you like an old friend, and the melodies of birds and the whisper of waterfalls soothe your soul."

Her voice was a tender echo of her memories.

Amara listened intently, her heart moved by Sakura's description. "I've heard of it," she said softly. "Wait—Asagiri … in Kai, correct?"

"No, it borders Kai. In Suruga," Sakura corrected, her eyes drifting as if visualizing the map.

Amara's reaction was immediate, her brows knitting.

"Has that warlord's reach extended to Suruga?" she asked, anxiety lacing her words, fearing the spread of conflict to her province.

Sakura shook her head.

"I know nothing of this warlord you mention. Only that the fear of something drove my parents to abandon me, much like Chiyo's tale. They cast me aside like a stranger, denying any bond we once shared. They acted as if they had never seen me before."

The conversation deepened, Amara pressing to learn more, until Yasuke's voice interrupted their moment, calling from a distance.

Amara reached for Sakura's hand, intending to lead her toward Yasuke, but Sakura resisted, pulling away sharply.

"Where are you taking me?" Sakura's voice quivered.

"To my Chichi-ue, Yasuke-sama, so you can share your story with him," Amara explained gently.

Sakura's resistance was unmistakable.

"No … I don't want. I … I just want to be left alone. You can't understand what it's like to be discarded. But perhaps you'll find out if your parents decide to abandon you without cause."

Her words held bitterness and pain.

Amara remained unshaken by Sakura's harsh words, understanding the depth of hurt behind them.

"I would hope my father would never do such a thing. And he might help you heal from what you've endured—or at least uncover the reasons behind it. Please, come with us," she urged again, her hand extended in a gesture of welcome and solidarity.

This time, Chiyo joined in, taking Sakura's other hand. Together, they stood by Sakura, a physical manifestation of the support and protection they offered. This gesture spoke volumes, offering Sakura the promise of assistance and the comfort of companionship.

Sakura more easily accepted the gesture when Chiyo joined in. Perhaps knowing that Chiyo had been abandoned was a help.

As they drew near to Yasuke, Amara, Chiyo, and Sakura moved with hesitation. Yasuke's always perceptive eyes immediately noted Sakura's unease. The young girl seemed to shrink back into herself, her eyes darting instinctively to the ground, her fingers nervously twisting the already frayed hem of her shirt.

Amara stepped in, her voice a bridge over the chasm of silence.

" Chichi-ue, meet Sakura," Amara said with a reassuring smile. "Her journey has been harsh, and she finds herself without a refuge. Her story resembles Chiyo's past."

Sakura remained silent, caught between the urge to share and the fear of being too vulnerable. Yasuke's eyes lingered on her, his nod conveying a promise of safety rather than a demand for her story.

Amara continued, " Chichi-ue, there are two more girls like Sakura who also seem lost and in need of help."

She did not say, "What can we do about them?" But the question still tainted the air anyway. Everyone knew it was there.

Without a moment's further delay, Chiyo's voice pierced the solemn atmosphere. "I'll go fetch them!" she declared.

Yasuke simply smiled. At this rate, they would soon have an orphanage. Still, he was glad to see the girls' sweet compassion.

With a swift turn, Chiyo set off to locate the other girls.

Yasuke and Amara turned their attention back to Sakura.

He noticed that Sakura's hands had started to tremble.

"Every person carries a story etched into their soul by their trials," he said, looking deep into the eyes of Sakura. "I am no different. You do not need to be afraid. Your journey has led you here, and if you're willing, it can lead to new beginnings. Our home is a place of healing and strength if you want it. You're not alone anymore, Sakura."

A faint smile blossomed on Sakura's face, kindled by Yasuke's assurance. Moments went by before Chiyo reemerged with an obvious expression of disappointment.

"I managed to speak with one of the girls," she proclaimed, her voice breaking as if she might start sobbing uncontrollably. "She is too frightened to come along, and the other one ran off!"

Yasuke nodded in his simple acceptance of the information and began to methodically place his supplies onto the wagon, making room for the trio of girls. With everyone aboard, they set off.

Leaving the marketplace behind, they made their way from the bustling market, the girls subdued by the sad loss of the others.

At a local izakaya nearby, three men shared a drink, their demeanor and attire suggesting a common military allegiance.

Their conversation halted abruptly as Yasuke and the girls passed by; one man, his sake cup paused midair, nudged his companion, nodding subtly toward Yasuke. "You see him? Who is that dark-skinned giant?" he inquired.

The one who seemed to lead their small band furrowed his brows, a spark of recognition flitting across his face.

"I cannot be certain, but … but … his stature is remarkable. Could he be? No … No … surely not," he said, more to himself than to his companions.

"And who might that be?" the third man pressed, leaning in with interest. "Of whom are you thinking?"

"Legends tell of a kuroi hada named Yasuke, who once served the Oda Nobunaga in Owari Province. His tale ended with Nobunaga's demise; he was believed to have perished alongside his lord."

With a final, lingering glance, the leader's eyes sharpened as if trying to pierce the growing distance between them and the wagon. He remained silent, lost in thought, the possibility of witnessing a figure from the annals of their nation's storied past leaving him momentarily adrift in a sea of wonder and doubt.

Yasuke, though silent, was fully aware of the men and their presence while gathering his items. His experienced eye, catching the casual stance and the men's uniform, identified them as scouts rather than frontline soldiers. These men were likely gathering intelligence, perhaps in preparation for something larger at play.

As they made their way back, the journey home was marked by a lightness that had not been present at Midoriya.

Slowly unwrapping the layers of her guarded demeanor, Sakura began to engage more openly with Amara and Chiyo.

She inquired about life at their home, to which the girls enthusiastically responded, promising her a taste of Yuki's renowned broth, which they proclaimed to rank among the best in Japan.

Yasuke's mind, however, was wandering to more pressing concerns. He was contemplating how Yuki would react to the addition of another dependent in their family.

Beyond the immediate practicalities, a deeper worry gnawed at him. If Sakura's past mirrored Chiyo's, then it could be a harbinger of conflict spreading to Suruga once again, a portent of bad things.

The thought weighed heavily on him, not just for his family's safety but also for the implications for the region's broader peace.

Meanwhile, back at their residence, Yuki was immersed in her routine of preparing the evening meal; her movements were rhythmic, but there was an undercurrent of unease.

The recent turmoil had also left a shadow over her usual tranquility, prompting her to cast wary glances out of the window at frequent intervals. She sought reassurance in her peaceful surroundings, vigilantly watching for signs of danger approaching their doorstep while Yasuke and the girls were away from the house.

As the evening meal neared readiness, Yasuke and the girls rounded the final hill, coming into view of their home.

Alerted by the familiar sounds of their approach, Yuki rushed to the window for confirmation. Upon sighting them, her heart swelled with relief, though the side-to-side bobbing of an additional head among them briefly caught her off guard. Without hesitation, she turned back to set an extra plate at the table for the unexpected guest.

The door burst open, Yasuke stepping in first, contentment in his demeanor. He enveloped Yuki in a welcoming embrace, then turned to introduce their guest.

"Yuki, this is …" he began, only to be interrupted by Amara and Chiyo's excited shouts, "Sakura!"

Their voices filled the room with joyous laughter.

"Well … Sakura, welcome!" Yuki responded, her tone full of warmth. "Please, come inside. I prepared a meal for you when I noticed an extra person in the wagon. See, I set out Sakura's plate!"

The evening unfolded quietly within the confines of their home, now sheltering five souls. The dinner table was a scene of relaxed ease, with the melody of slurping broth and the soft clinks of chopsticks against bowls dominating the ambiance.

A generous serving of rice accompanied the meal, offering everyone a simple yet undeniably profound comfort.

After dinner, Yasuke led Sakura to a cozy room she could call her own for the night. Amara and Chiyo, weary from the day's events, also sought the comfort of their beds, energy spent, and bellies full.

While the girls slept, Yasuke and Yuki lingered, delving into the day's revelations. Yuki broached the subject weighing on her mind.

"Are our fears now manifesting?" She paused before continuing, "I refrained from asking you during dinner, but does Sakura's tale echo Chiyo's past misfortunes?"

Yasuke nodded. "It seems likely," he admitted. "There were others as well. It appears many families are now disowning their daughters to evade the crippling daughter levy."

"Has that decree been enforced in Suruga as well?" asked Yuki.

"I'm not sure …"

"We would lay down our lives before forsaking Amara," shouted Yuki.

Yasuke paused, lost in thought, before responding.

"On our journey home, I reflected on the desperation of these families. In their minds, abandonment might seem more merciful than the grim alternatives. Unable to pay the levy, their daughters would be condemned to brothels or slave camps, their debts a chain binding them for years, destroying any hope of a dignified life."

With a resigned nod, Yuki acknowledged Yasuke's perspective, her expression shaded by the complexity of their situation.

As days unfolded into a calm routine, Sakura, to her relief, found herself becoming part of their daily existence, a stark contrast to the instability that had stalked her since her abandonment. The comfort of regular meals and the security of a reliable shelter brought her a tranquility long missed. Yet, her integration posed a subtle challenge to the household's routine, especially their unique training regimen.

The challenge of unveiling the true essence of their family life to Sakura weighed on Yasuke and Yuki. The atypical roles and skills Yuki and the girls had adopted strayed far from the conventional expectations of Japanese women of their era.

Uncertain about how Sakura might react or adapt to their distinctive way of life, Amara, always championing transparency, proposed they simply unveil their world to Sakura.

Hopefully, she might even express interest in joining their training.

Yasuke, however, harbored reservations. Observing Sakura's slender frame and her somewhat awkward gait—arms flailing slightly as she moved, and frequently stumbling over her own feet—he assessed her potential for the rigorous training they undertook.

His experienced eye, attuned to discerning a warrior's spirit, failed to see the makings of a fighter in her. Sakura embodied the essence of a traditional Japanese woman, her strengths lying in homemaking.

Therefore, Sakura carved her niche within the household, not on the training grounds but in the core of their home. She eagerly engaged in all the household duties, assisting with meal prep, and supporting Yuki in the diligent upkeep of the garden.

On one warm afternoon, while Amara and Chiyo pursued their training discreetly, Sakura walked the grounds to clear her mind.

Amara and Chiyo, fresh from their period of meditation, noticed her taking a stroll nearby. Their faces lit up with smiles as they approached, signaling their intent to join with friendly waves.

Sakura greeted them with a hug, her expression turning to one of curiosity almost immediately after.

"What do you two do every day for so long?" asked Sakura.

Chiyo glanced toward Amara, silently deferring the answer to her. Amara, taking a moment to formulate a response, finally said, "We assist my father with gathering supplies for our home."

"But at the same time every day?" Sakura probed further.

" Chichi-ue values routine," Amara said while gesturing toward their home. "Anyway, let's head back."

As they began to walk back, Sakura, initially matching their pace, suddenly came to a halt. A tense silence engulfed her as she stood rooted to the spot, her voice trembling.

"What is this?" she asked, her eyes wide with shock.

Amara and Chiyo turned to see what had caught Sakura's attention. They were met with the sight of the red ground, a somber reminder of the recent conflict. Though nature had begun to reclaim the site already, evidence of the battle remained unmistakably clear in the bloodstained, iron soil. The ensuing silence spoke volumes as all three girls were locked in a hypnotic stare at the earth.

Though typically almost brutally honest, Amara chose to maintain their untold story, recognizing the panic amassing in Sakura's eyes.

"Not long ago, Father returned from a hunt with boar and deer. He decided to prepare the animals there before bringing the meat inside," she explained. "I know, it looks terrible but believe me—"

Sakura's eyes remained locked on the ground, skepticism coloring her features. "Amara, I hold you in high regard, but I cannot accept your tale as truth. I am more aware than you seem to think."

"Why would you doubt me, Sakura? It's the truth," Amara insisted, though much uncertainty crept into her voice. She blushed.

"Because right there, I see evidence of human life," Sakura retorted, her finger trembling as she pointed to a spot a short distance away from the bloodstained earth. "Human life and death."

Following her direction, all three girls stared at a small, mutilated finger illuminated by the afternoon's light, a minuscule detail overlooked until now, due to the sun's perfect accusatory position.

A heavy sigh escaped Chiyo, signaling her resignation.

She nudged Amara with her elbow.

Amara, her stubbornness waning, decided it was time to unveil the truth to Sakura. "I am sorry for my untruth, Sakura. I hoped to spare you a bitter realization, that is all. But listen. Chiyo, my mother, and I diverge from the traditional path of Japanese women.

"You see, we are warriors, trained to defend our home, family, and honor. We stand up for those who cannot defend themselves."

Amara's voice echoed a solemn truth.

The surroundings fell silent, punctuated only by distant horses' neighs. Amara paused, allowing Sakura space to respond.

She remained silent.

"Your plight, Sakura, is filled with misfortune," Amara continued.

"Why do you say that?" Sakura finally spoke.

"Your experience mirrors Chiyo's. An evil daimyo seeks to conquer Japan, imposing harsh taxes to fund his campaign, including a levy on daughters. Families unable to pay are being forced to surrender their daughters into servitude or worse. If Suruga is under such threat, my family would rather die than forfeit our freedom. Sadly, Sakura, I doubt you can ever return home again."

Sakura's expression shifted to one of denial, her lips quivering in hesitation to accept Amara's grim outlook.

"Does this finger belong to one of the daimyo's soldiers?" she asked, all semblance of hope fading from her expression.

"No," Amara replied. "It belonged to a man who, along with four others, sought to harm us. We defended our family as necessary and cut them down. And we will do the same again when we need to."

Sakura's shock manifested in tears and trembling hands covering her face. "This … This isn't how women should act!" she sobbed. "Your … your family … You're all killers!"

"No," Amara countered firmly. "We are survivors. We did what we had to, to protect our home. Understand and accept this, Sakura. You can join us, and together, we can stand strong against any threat, even from that cruel daimyo."

"No! No …" Sakura protested, panic setting in. "I must leave here! I have to go home. I cannot live with you!"

As Sakura turned to flee, the wind intensified, carrying her desperation along with it.

"Wait, Sakura!" Chiyo called out, reaching out to her in vain.

"Let her go, Chiyo," Amara sighed deeply. "We did what we could. If she hates what we stand for, she will never accept us."

A chill of sorrow enveloped Amara and Chiyo as they turned back home, their spirits as heavy as the stormy atmosphere around.

Once again, Sakura found herself alone, adrift and tangled in a frenzy of emotions as she rushed through the forest.

Her quick steps made her oblivious to the gathering storm clouds, her sole focus on the turmoil within.

Hours passed, her swift pace carrying her back to Midoriya's center sooner than anticipated, her anxiety blinding her to the distance covered. The world seemed to darken around her, a reflection of her internal despair as she ventured beyond Midoriya, propelled by a desperate search for solace.

Hunger and exhaustion were mere shadows along her path, overpowered by a relentless drive for answers.

Five days later.

Amara and her family were immersed in a quiet celebration, marking Chiyo's birthday with a modest meal. The table boasted a selection of tai fish, its flesh kissed by flames and glazed with miso. A bowl of Ochazuke, with its comforting warmth of green tea poured over rice, complemented the meal, catering to Chiyo's fondness for rich flavors.

The celebration was subdued, yet Amara had sought to make it memorable for Chiyo with a thoughtful gesture. As the meal concluded, she presented Chiyo with a new kimono, symbolizing their bond and in acknowledgment of the day.

Despite the shadows of her past, it was apparent that Chiyo had found a new sense of belonging within this family, her former life a distant memory amidst the warmth of their company. The atmosphere in the household was notably uplifted, a shared sentiment of unity binding them closely for the first time in weeks.

With their meal concluded, the family opted to stroll outside, hoping to digest the abundant feast they had just indulged in.

As they stepped outside, the sight of two distant figures approaching momentarily stirred memories of the conflict that had shaken their peace not so long ago. Tension briefly held them in its grasp until the identities of the oncoming silhouettes became clear.

It was Sakura, and she was not alone.

By her side was the other young girl from Midoriya, the one who had slipped away from Chiyo's earlier attempt to reach out.

Amara's facial features wavered between hesitance and faint excitement. Yuki, embodying the warmth of a welcoming fireplace, smiled gently at the sight of Sakura and her newfound companion.

Yasuke, steadfast as always in his stoicism, showed no emotion, his demeanor as impenetrable as a fortress wall.

In stark contrast, Chiyo, on the other hand, was visibly upset by Sakura's return, her body tense with a rush of barely contained wrath.

Sakura's initial smile also faded swiftly, replaced by a scowl of apprehension at the sight of Chiyo's evident displeasure.

"Why have you returned?" Chiyo's voice, laden with accusation, pierced the tense air.

Caught off guard, Sakura's mouth opened to reply, yet Chiyo pressed on, undeterred.

"Answer me! Why are you back? You fled from here as if we were not good enough! Yet all we did was try for you."

Stammering, Sakura attempted to gather her thoughts. "I … I …"

"You spat in the face of the sanctuary offered by Amara. You rejected a place in this family," said a defiant Chiyo. "A family that would have embraced and safeguarded you the way they have me."

A devastated Sakura looked at Chiyo with complete shock.

"I was scared," Sakura confessed, her voice a mere whisper, betraying inner turmoil. "Unlike you and Amara, I'm not accustomed to such openness, such freedom."

A cold silence descended upon the girls, a tense calm mirroring the gentle arrival of dawn's first light.

Reflecting on her anger surge, Chiyo felt surprised by the intensity of her emotions toward Sakura. The acknowledgment of her birthday by Amara and Yuki had lifted her spirits to euphoric heights, a warmth and recognition she had never experienced with her own family. With her large eyes, Chiyo stared deep into Sakura's.

The few seconds seemed like minutes. Then, suddenly, the tension began to fade away; Sakura, with tears teetering on the brink of her eyelashes, extended an olive branch in the form of an embrace.

Without uttering a single word, Chiyo returned the embrace, her actions conveying forgiveness more eloquently than words could.

Yuki approached, her face illuminated by a gentle smile, heartened by the sight of the girls finding resolution and understanding among themselves. "Welcome back, Sakura," Yuki greeted warmly, her eyes shifting to the young girl by Sakura's side.

"And who might this be with you?"

"This is Ayame," Sakura introduced. "Say hello, Ayame …"

Ayame, showing deep respect, bowed gracefully to Yuki, inclining her torso at about thirty degrees in a formal keirei bow.

Not limiting her respect to Yuki alone, she extended the same courteous bow to Amara and Chiyo. Amara and Chiyo exchanged a quick glance at each other, a silent communication of surprise and curiosity, before returning Ayame's bow with equal respect.

Sakura began to unravel the story of her fortuitous encounter with Ayame; it had been during her poignant return journey through Midoriya after a heart-wrenching visit to her parents' home.

Yasuke, having observed the introductions from a distance, finally approached the group, his presence commanding yet reassuring.

Sakura unfolded the tale of her family's rejection, a narrative marked by her father's stern refusal and her mother's silent tears.

Sakura's own experience now confirmed the harsh reality that Amara and Chiyo had previously laid bare.

Her father, amidst sobs, had revealed the grim reality: Lord Hideaki's bushi had not only encroached upon Shinano but had also breached the vulnerable borders of Suruga.

With a heavy heart, Sakura recounted her father's account of imposing warriors on horseback, their banners flying as they scoured the village, enforcing a draconian levy on families with daughters.

Those unable to meet the tax faced the unthinkable: their daughters would be seized to settle the dues.

As he implored her to flee, her father's tearful face was a sight Sakura had never witnessed, revealing the depth of his desperation and love. This pivotal moment reshaped her understanding, recognizing her departure as an act of love rather than of rejection.

Motivated by a newfound mindset and the protective embrace she had previously experienced, Sakura chose to return, seeking refuge and solidarity. Her chance encounter with Ayame in Midoriya had blossomed into an alliance forged from shared vulnerabilities.

As Sakura and Ayame shared tales, the resonance with Chiyo's past underscored the harrowing pattern emerging across their lands.

Sakura's expression of hopeful anticipation conveyed her earnest desire for forgiveness as she looked toward Amara and her family. A sigh of relief was observable in her demeanor as she firmly grasped Ayame's hand.

Then, she turned toward Yasuke with a request of sincerity.

"Your kindness opened your doors to me recently," Sakura began, her voice steady yet filled with humility. "I beg you, grant us—myself and Ayame—the same sanctuary once again."

The silence that followed was deafening, all eyes fixed on Yasuke, whose penetrating stare assessed the weary pair before him.

After a moment that seemed to stretch into eternity, Yasuke finally voiced his decision.

"Life's currents have brought you back to our home," he began. "You shall find shelter under our roof, yet it comes with the expectation of contributing to our collective purpose. Are you both ready to embrace the responsibilities accompanying our way of life?"

Sakura and Ayame, fortified by an inner strength contrasting with their outward gentleness, eagerly affirmed their readiness.

They gave a determined nod in unison.

Ayame then spoke, her voice never faltering.

"My wish is for peace and to offer my efforts toward safeguarding this sanctuary against the encroaching threats."

Yasuke responded to Ayame's declaration with a thoughtful nod, a silent acknowledgment that he accepted her show of commitment.

He then addressed both of them once again with a seriousness underscoring the importance of his ensuing words.

"I want to make something clear: we do not seek violence or conflict." He locked eyes with Ayame to emphasize his point.

"Yet, should adversity dare to approach our doorstep again, rest assured we will answer the door and never cower within. We will meet our assailants. Commit to the defense of this family and our land, and in turn, find protection within its bounds," he concluded.

Yasuke's clenched fist symbolized the fervor behind his words.

Ayame's spirit surged upon hearing Yasuke's impassioned speech, her eagerness to embrace the forthcoming challenges visible in her vigorous nodding and restless demeanor.

Seeing Ayame's fervor, Amara mirrored her enthusiasm with a sly grin, their shared energy apparent.

Yasuke then shifted his focus to Sakura, who, despite her towering stature amongst the girls, contrasted sharply with Ayame's warrior-like readiness. It was clear to him, as it had been from their first meeting, that Sakura's path lay not in the art of combat but elsewhere within the folds of their household.

"I've always been the one more likely to trip over my own feet than to land a successful strike," Sakura admitted with a hint of shy self-deprecation. "Even as a child, I struggled with coordination. My mother used to say I could trip over air."

A sheepish smile crossed her face.

"Yet, I see the strength and unity in this household. I see the seamless way in which everyone contributes, especially Yuki, whose efforts turn this house into a home. I may not wield a sword, but I can ensure that your … our home remains a sanctuary, lightening Yuki's load so she may dedicate more time to safeguarding and training. Would my contribution in this manner be of value here?"

Sakura's offer was sincere, her willingness to find her place within their unique family clearly ringing out.

Yasuke responded with a nod, acknowledging the fairness and value of Sakura's proposition. "Your assistance in maintaining the home is valuable and will be welcomed. Then we will make the necessary arrangements for your and Ayame's accommodation."

Chiyo, her earlier tensions forgotten, was overjoyed, along with Amara, at the prospect of expanding their family.

Their laughter and playful running around the yard were evidence of their happiness and acceptance of Sakura and Ayame.

Yasuke and Yuki exchanged a look of quiet pleasure before turning toward the house, contemplating the adjustments needed.

They would welcome their new members in every way possible.

CHAPTER TWELVE

The Right Hand of God

(神の右手)

Sakura's recanting of her father's story was an accurate account of the extent of his knowledge. As far as her father knew, the daimyo's men had just made it to Shinano and slowly penetrated the vast rural village of Asagiri. In actuality, however, Hideaki's bushi had already been in Shinano for three months. A small outfit of twenty Ashigaru warriors and two samurai monitored their small control over Shinano, which allowed them to perform surveillance and reconnaissance on Suruga.

In a normal situation, Yoshinori would've been right there in Suruga, leading reconnaissance efforts.

However, this time, his father had other plans for the young, fearless leader in a strategy that could reshape Japan forever.

As the Tokugawa Shogunate continued to rise—emerging victoriously by neutralizing continuous threats of rising daimyos jockeying for power—the shogun's awareness started to fall on Lord Hideaki's activities and his successful occupation of several provinces. Knowledgeable of this unwanted attention, Lord Hideaki felt it was time to gather political alliances to strengthen his efforts.

Lord Hideaki and Yoshinori turned their political strategy toward the province of Kai. Due to its strategic importance, Kai was a hotly contested region not ruled by a single daimyo.

However, a powerful and prominent daimyo named Takeda Torao had a strong influence over Kai. Lord Takeda Torao commanded an army of over seven thousand men.

In addition, Lord Takeda had two unwed daughters.

Lord Hideaki, in all his strategic wisdom, felt he could bridge an alliance with Lord Takeda by having Yohinori marry one of Lord Takeda's daughters. Ultimately, this alliance would give Lord Hideaki access to a bigger army to rise against the Tokugawa Shogunate.

An alliance would be monumental for both parties.

Both daimyos understood that, but they also understood that at a moment's notice, either of them could betray the other.

It would be a smart yet delicate strategy. Lord Hideaki was cunning and a master of these dangerous games of power and alliances; he always navigated with a keen willingness.

The meetings between him and Lord Takeda Torao were more about social camaraderie than political strategy.

Amidst his firearms dealings with the Portuguese, Lord Hideaki became introduced to tobacco, a novel pleasure being given as a token of goodwill by his European partners. The tobacco, presented in abundance, became a point of relaxation and intrigue for both daimyos, though it was Lord Takeda who developed a particular fondness for it. Thus, gatherings were marked by rooms clouded with their kiseru pipes' smoke, creating an atmosphere of contemplation and restful leisure amidst the rendezvous' political undertones.

Previous meetings had taken place in Totomi, within a small compound erected by Lord Hideaki since the occupation.

Despite its size, the compound vividly mirrored the daimyo's darker proclivities. It was dotted with giant stone fire pits, not for warmth but for torment. These pits became stages for the Lord's burgeoning fascination with suffering. Enemies, rebellious slaves, and even pregnant mistresses fell victim to these pits, subjected to torments that still could not satiate Lord Hideaki's cruel appetite.

Lord Hideaki found a perverse pleasure in the spectacle of agony, especially when he was its architect, revealing a sinister aspect of his rule that extended beyond the battlefield into the depths of cruelty.

Though notorious for his ruthlessness in battle, Lord Takeda Torao did not share Lord Hideaki's predilection for torture.

While Takeda's campaigns had led to the demise of many, he preferred the swiftness of the sword over any prolonged suffering. To him, torment and torture were unnecessary hindrances, a distraction from the more pressing goal of victory and expansion.

Committed to forge a political alliance of mutual benefit, the two lords agreed to a significant meeting, distinct from their prior casual encounters. This gathering was to be centered around concrete discussions of strategy and alliance, marking a departure from the conviviality characterizing their previous meetings.

Five Weeks Earlier.

The venue for this crucial meeting had been Kai, selected for its strategic importance and Takeda's influence in the area.

Lord Takeda, known for his refined tastes, hosted the meeting at his compound, a grand and nearly impregnable fortress stretching over two hundred yards. This setting, providing a stark contrast to the more austere ambiance of their previous interactions, underscored the gravity of their awaited discussions.

As dawn unfolded over Kai, the grandiose corridors of Lord Takeda Torao's fortress were alive with palpable tension and expectancy. With the morning light forming stretched shadows behind them, Lord Hideaki, his son Yoshinori, and the elite warriors of the Iron Bushi made their grand entrance.

Upon their arrival, they were immediately greeted by the fortress's caretakers, who took the reins of their horses as the group dismounted, their awe evident at the fortress's imposing stature.

"Remarkable," Lord Hideaki murmured to Yoshinori, who nodded in agreement, equally struck by the fortress's magnificence.

Together, they advanced through the fortress's vast halls to the grand Shuden, where Lord Takeda awaited their conference.

The servant slid the doors open with practiced grace as they approached, revealing the grandeur within.

"My lord awaits," the servant announced, guiding them forward with a wave of his hand.

"Lord Hideaki," boomed a commanding voice from the hall's heart. "Please, join me," Lord Takeda invited with open arms.

"Thank you," Lord Hideaki responded, appreciatively glancing around. "Your estate is truly magnificent."

Lord Takeda offered a knowing smile.

"This fortress is a testimony to my might, not bestowed by any shogun or emperor, but earned through the loyalty and bravery of my warriors," he declared, packing tobacco into his kiseru pipe with a focus that suggested it was his precious ritual.

Despite the grandeur of the gesture, Lord Hideaki gently refused the pipe. "While I value your hospitality, Lord Takeda, I fear indulging might distract me from the crucial matters at hand."

"Nonsense," Lord Takeda countered robustly. "By the time you leave, we will have reached an agreement, one way or another. Our discussions will find their conclusion, pipe or no pipe."

Accepting this, Lord Takeda prepared another two pipes, one for himself and one for Yoshinori as servants seamlessly entered, filling ceramic cups with sake.

Lord Hideaki exchanged a glance with Yoshinori, a look of mild annoyance at the additional formalities, signaling his eagerness to focus on their visit's purpose.

For around half an hour, Lords Hideaki and Takeda exchanged pleasantries while Yoshinori, slightly more relaxed after his third cup of sake, observed silently. By now, the room was filled with the rich scent of incense, a subtle veil over the growing tobacco smell.

Lord Hideaki took the lead in the conversation, his tone respectful, recognizing Takeda's significant sway over Kai.

"Your control over Kai and command of a mighty force are commendable, Lord Takeda. In these uncertain times, your leadership stands as a pillar of strength," he stated, laying the groundwork for his forthcoming proposition.

Lord Takeda, seasoned and cautious, acknowledged the compliment with a thoughtful nod.

He countered, "And your tactical advancements, Lord Hideaki, have not gone unnoticed. Your conquests boast of your formidable ambition and strength." He was recognizing Hideaki's achievements while also alluding to the potential threat they represented.

The conversation pivoted to the heart of their meeting: a proposal aimed at consolidating their power against the shogunate's growing influence. "I propose we form an alliance," Hideaki declared, lifting his cup of sake as a symbol of his earnest proposal. "My son Yoshinori—who has proven his mettle and leadership time and again—marrying into your esteemed family would solidify our clans' union, intertwining our fates and strengths."

Lord Takeda pondered the offer, his face betraying nothing of his inner calculations. Although he had anticipated this proposal, understanding Hideaki's character over their interactions had made him wary. The idea of leveraging one of his daughters in a political marriage was not new. Still, the thought of an alliance with Hideaki—a man of unchecked ambition and ruthlessness—demanded careful thought and would not be decided in haste or under pressure.

"Such an alliance could indeed present a formidable challenge to the shogunate," Takeda said, his voice betraying a slight caution. "However, alliances, much like the fleeting beauty of our cherry blossoms, can be ephemeral, prone to be swayed by fate and ambition. How can we ensure this bond remains loyal?"

Leaning in, Hideaki met Takeda's gaze with a firm intensity.

"At the heart of any alliance lies trust. I offer not only my son but also my unwavering loyalty. United, we can redefine the political landscape of Japan, propelling our clans to unprecedented prominence. Our allied forces would stand as a beacon against any opposition."

Lord Takeda stood, pipe in hand, smoke swirling around him.

He fixed Lord Hideaki with a piercing gaze, exhaling a thick plume before speaking. "Lord Hideaki, my tastes are as lavish as they are varied. My pleasures range from the company of women to the joys of sake and, most recently, tobacco, thanks to our dealings.

"Commanding a powerful army grants me the luxury to further indulge in these desires, a sentiment shared by my warriors. We rule with unflinching authority, maintaining our grip on what we hold dear. Yet, I've always seen Japan as unpredictable, akin to a courtesan too easily swayed by temptation. The loyalty of this land, like that of a paid whore, is fickle and fraught with betrayal."

Lord Hideaki and Yoshinori exchanged glances, puzzled by Lord Takeda's candid metaphor and unsure of the direction in which the discussion was heading. Hideaki was intent on seeking clarity.

"Once again, with all due res—"

Takeda's continuation cut him short with a forthright declaration.

"Understand this. I harbor no ambitions to rule Japan in its entirety, unlike you. Should our alliance proceed, you need not fear any semblance of disloyalty from me. My aspirations do not extend that far beyond my current dominions. I offer my support, envisioning you as a god, and I will be God's right hand, supplying warriors to bolster your ranks against the shogunate."

With that, Lord Takeda set aside his pipe and gestured toward the entrance, prompting Lord Hideaki and Yoshinori to turn their attention to the figure making her way into the room.

A dignified woman, clad in a luxurious black and gold kimono, entered the room, bringing with her a commanding presence. Her confident stride was as telling as her attire, yet her gaze remained modestly lowered as she approached, taking her place beside Lord Takeda. With a respectful bow to the lord and then to the guests, her silent introduction spoke volumes of her upbringing and stature.

"Gentlemen," Takeda announced. "This is my esteemed daughter, Tomoe. In her, I see the zenith of my lineage, surpassing even my own son in value. Tomoe's strategic prowess and valor have been instrumental in my victories, her sharp intellect fortifying our clan's might. Beyond her tactical acumen, her poise, beauty, and honor elevate our family's renown. Her alliance in marriage will not only augment your forces but also enhance your clan's moral fabric. She is the epitome of what a noble wife should be."

Yoshinori, somewhat inebriated by imbibing too much sake, looked at Tomoe with an expression between awe and curiosity. His gaze lingered on her, reminiscent of a hawk observing its quarry.

Meanwhile, Lord Hideaki's reaction was more subdued.

While the proposal of alliance and marriage to Takeda's daughter aligned with his ambitions—granting him access to Takeda's elite forces and bolstering their clans' unity—Hideaki was acutely aware of the price such an alliance might demand.

Despite the strategic advantages, he recognized the complexities and potential sacrifices involved in thus intertwining their destinies.

Lord Hideaki, seeking a perspective from Yoshinori, noticed his son's focus had grown dulled by the sake, rendering his insight less than helpful at the moment. Turning his attention back to Lord Takeda, he observed the daimyo enjoying another bout of tobacco.

The room was once again filling with thick, curling smoke.

"A most generous proposal indeed," Lord Hideaki acknowledged, his voice measured.

In response, Lord Takeda acknowledged the compliment with a nod, his pipe momentarily poised in midair.

A quiet moment passed, during which Tomoe lifted her gaze to study the guests. Lord Hideaki, catching sight of her, was struck by her refined features; her delicate nose and the intensity of her gaze only heightened her allure, causing Hideaki to ponder the depth of Lord Takeda's proposition further.

"Such offerings to the Iron Bushi, and especially, the betrothal of your esteemed daughter Tomoe to my son, Yoshinori, represent significant commitments on your part. What concessions, then, do you envisage from my clan and myself?" inquired Lord Hideaki.

After a pause to consider his response, Lord Takeda said, "Your successes are commendable in their own right and likely achievable with or without my support. Yet, with my assistance, victory is assured. This alliance ensures we both stand on the favorable side of history. It is to our considerable and undeniable advantage."

"Your confidence is reassuring," Hideaki remarked, acknowledging the vote of trust.

Lord Takeda leaned in slightly, his expression turning serious.

"My condition is straightforward: I seek a share in the spoils from each victory, tax, and conquest."

"Every single one?" Hideaki retorted in a tone of disbelief as he locked eyes with Lord Takeda. It was a tense and serious moment.

As Lord Takeda released another stream of smoke from his kiseru, he weighed his next words carefully, mindful of the delicate balance of power between him and Lord Hideaki.

Recognizing the unpredictability of Hideaki's temperament, he carefully crafted his reply.

"Lord Hideaki, I mean no disrespect, but the contributions I seek are but a mere droplet in the vast ocean of advantage my forces will bestow upon your conquests. This is especially true for the inevitable confrontation with the shogunate. To wage such a war, your treasury must be as bountiful as Mount Fuji. My daughter shall be instrumental in this regard with her exceptional acumen."

Lord Hideaki let out a short, scornful laugh.

"Entrust your progeny with managing my wealth? A convenient arrangement for you, is it not?" he replied with much skepticism.

"Our progeny," Lord Takeda corrected with firmness. "Once she marries into your family, she becomes our shared responsibility. I would stake my life on her integrity, prepared to take her head myself should she betray our trust. Tomoe possesses unmatched financial acumen within Kai, navigating numbers with the finesse and balance of any seasoned Noh performer."

Lord Takeda then sweetened the deal.

"Your son, the valiant and tactical Yoshinori, shall receive a substantial fief: one-fourth of Kai's land will be his to govern. You will have the authority to legislate and levy taxes on its yields."

The proposal visibly altered Lord Hideaki's demeanor.

Initial skepticism gave way to a cautious optimism.

The comprehensive nature of Lord Takeda's offer, blending martial alliance with economic benefits and familial bonds, presented a compelling, albeit unexpected, opportunity for mutual benefit.

"I appreciate your offer not being slight," Lord Hideaki began, his voice showing its calculated restraint. "Your proposal warrants thorough contemplation. I shall require the evening to deliberate on your bounteous proposition."

With a graceful gesture from Lord Takeda, the room quickly filled with servants.

"I anticipated your need for reflection. Accommodations have been prepared for your quiet enjoyment and consideration. And should it please you, arrangements for entertainment can be made," Takeda offered, alluding to the potential company of a courtesan.

"That will suffice," Hideaki acknowledged with a nod.

Lord Takeda's expression then hinted at an additional strategic layer yet to be discussed. "Before you are shown to your quarters, let us not overlook Suruga," he introduced, steering the conversation toward new territory.

"Suruga? A land of modest means, filled with farmers and women, hardly the nectar of the flower," Hideaki responded.

What would be the province's strategic value?

Takeda's eyes sparkled with the wisdom of a seasoned tactician, though he was clearly taken aback by the acerbic comment.

"You underestimate the value of Suruga's rice paddies. They are not mere plots of land but fields of an endless quilt of green, stitched through with threads of fortune. Imposing a levy on rice production could unlock a wealth of resources."

Lord Hideaki found himself deeply engrossed in thought, his fingers unconsciously stroking his beard. Indeed, Takeda's insights had cast Suruga in a new light, sparking both excitement and a pang of regret for not having recognized its potential himself.

Ceasing his contemplative gesture, Hideaki turned to his hosts with a strategic augmentation to the conversation. "Given Suruga's demographics, it also presents an opportune moment to reinforce the daughter levy. The establishment of additional brothels could significantly amplify the revenue generated from taxes."

Then, Lord Hideaki paused thoughtfully, his gaze shifting to Yoshinori, whose subtle nod affirmed his agreement with his father's words. Turning back to Lord Takeda and the assembled servants, Lord Hideaki continued, "As I stated. I will take the remainder of the day to deliberate and confer with my son and trusted advisors."

The room filled with a respectful silence as Lord Hideaki's reiteration settled over the gathering, marking a moment of purposeful pause in the intricate dance of alliance and ambition.

CHAPTER THIRTEEN

A Sparrow among Crows

(カラスの中のスズメ)

Six Weeks Later

The last stubborn drizzles of rain tapered off, signaling the end of late spring. Within the tranquil abode, each member settled comfortably into their roles. Ambitious by nature, Ayame eagerly joined Amara, Chiyo, and Yasuke in their rigorous training and meditation routines.

Sakura, fully mindful of her limitations in physical combat, dedicated herself to the upkeep of the home.

She assisted Yuki in preparing meals, maintaining impeccable order, and tending to the garden. Occasionally, she would participate in the training sessions, but her lack of coordination often led her to bow out early. Nevertheless, she recognized the value of engaging as much as she could, gaining much from their sessions.

Gradually, Sakura grew adept at anticipating how Yuki preferred the garden to adapt to the changing climate, skillfully arranging the plants so that they would thrive in each season.

One day, as Sakura rearranged some flowering plants, Yuki approached her from behind, observing her work.

"Sakura, your meticulousness in this craft is admirable," Yuki complimented, observing Sakura's work over her shoulder.

Startled at first, Sakura quickly regained composure and responded with a bow. "Thank you, Okāsan. I aspire to emulate your elegance, though I doubt I can ever match it."

"Oh, don't sell yourself short, Sakura. And thank you, but I'm hardly the model of traditional Japanese femininity—at least, that's what my father and brother would say," Yuki confessed, her gaze drifting momentarily before returning to Sakura.

"You've arranged these blooms just as I would have. I'm so grateful and fortunate to have your help."

Yuki leaned in to inspect the floral arrangement more closely.

"Yes! … You've done a very thorough job here, Sakura. Allow me to suggest just a few adjustments."

"I would be honored," Sakura replied, eager to learn.

Yuki picked up one of the flowers, admiring it closely.

"These are magnificent specimens. Notice how gracefully they stand on their slender sturdy stems, their delicate pink and white petals like fine art, with vibrant centers of golden yellow."

"Such poetic imagery, Okāsan," Sakura remarked. "What are these called?"

"These are Anemone of Japan, though I've always called them my little shadow blossoms," Yuki shared with a smile.

"Shadow blossoms?" Sakura echoed, intrigued.

"Yes, and that brings me to a small oversight in your otherwise flawless layout. These blossoms thrive best in shade, yet they're currently in full sunlight. We should move them near the house where the roof's edge casts permanent shadows, ensuring they flourish in darkness come late summer. That's why I adore these blooms, since they are powerful through darkness."

Their eyes met, sharing a moment of mutual appreciation and understanding.

"I look forward to seeing them at their peak," said Sakura enthusiastically. "Let's move them now!" She laughed lightly as they both set to work repositioning the plants.

As the mid-morning sun crept across the training field, Ayame's eagerness and swift learning curve were on full display.

She sparred with Chiyo, despite consistently being outmatched; her competitive spirit was burgeoning, her skills sharpening with each encounter. Meanwhile, Amara often completed her exercises sooner than the others, taking time afterward to observe and assist Yasuke in coaching Ayame and Chiyo.

"They're making impressive progress," Yasuke remarked to Amara as they watched from a distance.

Amara, her eyes shimmering with gratitude, nodded in agreement.

"Thank you for giving them a chance to stay," she said. "I can't bear to think of what might have happened to them. Orphans caught in slavery or worse, left to continue to fend for themselves out there."

Yasuke nodded, his expression masked in solemn agreement.

He shared Amara's relief, yet his mind was consumed with broader political concerns. *How soon might Lord Hideaki move on Suruga? And what of the shogunate—will it manage to thwart his advances?*

These thoughts lingered as he watched the young trainees.

The uncertainty of the times underscored the urgency of their training. Each needed to be prepared to defend.

Yasuke's mind wandered momentarily before announcing his plans, his tone shifting as he looked around. "I am heading to Midoriya to gather more supplies and provisions," he said, his voice reflecting a sudden urgency to divert his thoughts.

"Should I accompany you?" Amara asked, her voice tinged with a hopefulness that suggested she already anticipated his answer.

Typically, Yasuke would respond instantly with a no, but this time, he hesitated. This pause was uncharacteristic. Perhaps it was the lingering oppressive political tensions on his mind, or maybe, just maybe, he realized the comfort in having company.

After a brief moment of contemplation, he made his decision.

"No," he finally responded, more gently than usual. "I plan to be back before the evening meal."

"We'll be here waiting," Amara replied, offering a reassuring smile.

As Yasuke turned to leave, the thunderous clacking of Chiyo and Ayame's bokkens gradually diminished behind him, their sounds blending into the backdrop of another rigorous training session.

As Yasuke emerged from the dense forest, the modest charm of Midoriya unfolded before him. While it lacked the grandeur of the larger cities he had visited across Japan, the settlement held a special place in his heart for its steady growth and the warm acceptance he received there as a dark-skinned foreigner.

Yasuke made his way through the usual stops within the settlement, but he couldn't help but notice a stark change in the usual lively atmosphere. The market stalls, usually abuzz with activity, were now hushed, only a handful of locals engaged in quiet conversations.

Once filled with the sounds of life, the streets were now mostly silent, broken only by the occasional laughter of children at play.

After securing the needed supplies to his wagon, Yasuke prepared to leave. As he maneuvered toward the settlement's edge, a voice halted him. "Yasuke!"

Yasuke paused, turning slowly to face the direction of the call.

"Ah, I thought you might have been him!" a man said, wearing a warrior's kimono. "The Kuroi Hada of Lord Nobunaga," the man continued, nodding to two companions by his side.

Yasuke remained silent, and turned back, urging his horse down his usual path. To his relief, the men did not follow.

Instead, they walked in the opposite direction.

The morning breeze played with the horse's mane as Yasuke rode, his gaze lost in its flowing movements. The world around him seemed to slow, his thoughts overrun by reflections and concerns that stretched far beyond the serene landscape.

In nearly a decade in Suruga, recognition has escaped me, or perhaps indifference has cloaked their eyes. Who were those men? he pondered, unusually troubled by the peculiar encounter.

Yasuke recalled a similar insignia on the men's kimonos, one he had seen weeks ago during their first meeting with Sakura in Midoriya. This detail nagged at him, igniting a sense of caution.

Abruptly, he halted his horse, intuition telling him he was not alone. With careful slowness, he looked back, scanning the path he had just traveled. His suspicions were confirmed; the same men from earlier were now discreetly trailing him on horseback.

Their presence was a silent threat hanging like a dense fog.

Yasuke's instincts warned him of danger, a familiar unease settling deep in his gut like an anchor in stormy seas.

Weary of the endless battles that had marred his soul, he braced for what might unfold. With a confident turn of his horse, he faced the men, his steely gaze fixed on the apparent leader.

"Is there something I can assist you with?" Yasuke inquired, his voice steady and devoid of warmth.

"Yasuke, the tales of your exploits have reached far and wide. The former slave who became Nobunaga's esteemed bodyguard—it's an honor to finally meet you," the leader declared with a veneer of respect.

Yasuke did not return the man's salutation; his piercing look cut through the late morning chill. His suspicions remained.

"Perhaps this isn't him," muttered one of the men uncertainly.

"It's definitely him," the leader affirmed loudly, ensuring Yasuke overheard. "After all, there was only one dark-skinned man allowed in all of Japan, spared because he was a foreigner, not deemed worthy of a samurai's death. Ordered to leave Japan … and yet here you are, hidden away in this secluded village. Surprising that your presence here has gone unreported so far."

Yasuke remained composed, his expression unchanging as he repeated his question with a stern, unyielding tone.

"I asked, may I assist you with anything?"

The leader scoffed dismissively.

"Let's not be hasty, Yasuke. Think of this as an opportunity to reclaim your legacy under Lord Hideaki's banner," he proposed, the promise of power hanging in the air like a veiled sword. "I am a teisatsu gashira, and along with my scouts, I am conducting reconnaissance in Suruga under the command of Lord Hideaki."

At the mention of Lord Hideaki, Yasuke's demeanor shifted subtly from guarded vigilance to alert curiosity.

His eyes, previously narrow slits of focused intention, now reflected intrigue. The tension between Yasuke and the scout leader thickened as they stood under the open sky of Suruga.

"So, you comprehend the prosperity and authority my lord will bring to these lands?" the leader asked pointedly. "Perhaps this is your chance to serve the true unifier of Japan."

Reflecting on the past decade—a life interwoven with bonds he cherished deeply, with Yuki and the girls engraved in his memory—Yasuke's response carried an air of finality.

"Your observation was correct, I am indeed Yasuke," he declared, his voice firm. "But the Yasuke you speak of is no more. I serve no lord now, nor do I wish to do so, ever again."

The leader, affirming Yasuke's identity to his men, persisted.

"There was never any doubt you were him. Yet regardless of your readiness or otherwise, Lord Hideaki's dominion over this land is inevitable. Given your renowned past, a generous fief might be yours should you pledge your service."

Yasuke's lips curled into a rare smile.

"Should your Lord Hideaki claim these lands, I'll face that when the time comes. Until then, I respectfully decline your offer."

The scout leader's demeanor soured, his face twisting in disdain.

Ryota Hojo, his and his clan's name known in the neighboring Izu Province for prowess and loyalty to Lord Hideaki, was not one to take rejection lightly. He paced irritably, all earlier cordiality dissolved.

He now eyed Yasuke with bare-faced contempt.

"So, you willingly served as Nobunaga's dog without any qualms?" he sneered, the venom in his words matched only by the spittle flying from his lips. "You're no true warrior, Yasuke, let alone a samurai. Just a spectacle Nobunaga flaunted. And now, you dare carry two swords. Can you even wield them?"

Yasuke regarded the men with a scornful shake of his head, his patience waning. He dismounted his horse with deliberate slowness, every movement measured. "Unfortunately for you, the only way to prove whether I can use these swords is to show you."

The underlying threat was clear in his voice.

His initial unease had crystallized into certainty. Blood would soon be staining the earth of Suruga.

Yasuke was acutely aware of the daunting odds stacked against him. He was outnumbered, the specter of death looming ominously.

His seasoned eye discerned the severity of the situation.

He could skillfully handle and overpower one or two of these foes; however, a collective of this caliber posed a genuine, life-threatening challenge. Their garb and weaponry were signs of their lethal prowess, branding them seasoned adversaries.

"Look, Yasuke, we didn't come here seeking a fight," Ryota called out, his voice quivering. "But your refusal leaves me no choice. Once Lord Hideaki and Lord Takeda hear of your stubbornness, I'll likely be ordered to bring them your head."

Ryota's voice began trembling.

Although skeptical of the legendary tales shrouding Yasuke, Ryota saw this as a chance to elevate his own status. *Defeating Yasuke would immortalize my name across the regions,* he mused silently.

The warriors unsheathed their swords and began circling Yasuke, employing a tactical flanking maneuver that left Ryota in the center.

Yasuke, well-versed in countless battle techniques from his days serving Lord Nobunaga, was unfazed. He gripped Kurokaze's hilt as if the weapon were a fond old friend, feeling the handle's familiar warmth as he drew his beloved katana.

With a swift motion, he unsheathed his second sword, the blade catching the sunlight menacingly as the men closed in.

"You face certain death, Yasuke," Ryota taunted.

Like a pair of predators, Ryota and one of his men swooped in with a ferocious assault from the off.

Yasuke's response was swift and instinctive, his dual katanas a blur of defense and counterattack. The clash of steel was unrelenting, each combatant pushing the boundaries of their speed and skill.

Despite their best efforts, Yasuke's impressive strength repelled them time and again, the thrill of battle coursing through his veins.

A momentary lull fell over the battlefield as both sides caught their breath. The warriors, though younger, showed signs of exhaustion, already, their chests heaving with each breath.

Yasuke, despite his age, managed to mask his own fatigue—an art he had mastered over his years of combat, delivering a distinct psychological advantage. Impressed yet wary opponents circled Yasuke, each waiting for an opening.

Ryota recognized that overpowering the dominant Yasuke would require a coordinated assault from all three men. Yet, the complexity of orchestrating such an attack without harming each other due to Yasuke's impressive agility and size posed a real challenge. As they prepared for another charge, Ryota and his warriors accepted the truth that the legendary tales about the black samurai were accurate.

The men communicated with military precision, using hand signals to coordinate a staggered attack pattern, intent on exhausting Yasuke. Ryota led the first attack with precise timing, followed swiftly by the second warrior. As soon as the second retreated, the third man attacked from the opposite direction, like a swift gust of wind.

Yasuke skillfully dodged or parried each threatening strike, but the relentless sequence barely gave him a moment to recover.

This rhythm started to show promise in wearing him down, forcing Yasuke to adopt a more defensive posture.

As the once-bright morning sun became obscured by gathering clouds, the atmosphere seemed to mirror the dire situation in which Yasuke found himself. The air felt thunder-laden, stormy.

In a brief lapse, Ryota managed to nick Yasuke's chest, drawing first blood. However, this did not deter Yasuke. When the third assailant overextended, Yasuke seized the moment to incapacitate him with a powerful kick to the knee, causing him to buckle in pain.

This momentarily disrupted the trio's rhythm, giving Yasuke a crucial recovery moment. But as the three regrouped and charged again, Yasuke stumbled on uneven ground, falling backward, and dropping his swords. Seizing what they thought was a decisive moment, the warriors advanced to deliver the final blow.

But, unexpectedly, a blade from nowhere pierced through the chest of the third man, fatally striking him as he crumpled, blood spraying across Yasuke's face. To his shock, Yasuke recognized Yuki's brother, Hideyoshi, holding the other end of the weapon.

Springing to his feet with astonishing quickness, Yasuke reclaimed his swords. Ryota quickly refocused his attention on Yasuke, and the other attacker engaged Hideyoshi, who, despite not being a seasoned warrior, somehow managed to hold his own.

Knowing he needed to end the fight quickly, Yasuke blocked Ryota's fierce katana swings with Kurokaze, counterattacking, plunging his second blade deep into Ryota's abdomen.

Ryota's sword fell, sticking blade first into the earth.

With a swift kick, Yasuke dislodged Ryota from his blade, allowing his body to drop like a sack of rice.

Rushing to aid Hideyoshi, Yasuke witnessed him sustain a severe slash across the chest. With a mighty leap, Yasuke decapitated the attacker in a decisive swipe, turning in time to catch Hideyoshi.

"Are you all right, Hideyoshi?" Yasuke asked, sincerely concerned.

Hideyoshi, pale and bleeding, managed a faint response. "Yasuke ... I am fine. But are you all right, Yasuke?"

He must have noticed the blood seeping from Yasuke's wound.

"I'm fine also, thanks to you," Yasuke reassured, quickly assessing Hideyoshi's injuries. They were grave. "Let's get you to safety."

Knowing the severity of Hideyoshi's condition, Yasuke helped him onto his horse, walking slowly beside it as they made their way back. Hideyoshi, struggling with each breath, expressed gratitude.

"Thank you Yasuke! I ... I am sorry for returning to Midoriya!" said Hideyoshi in a shaky voice.

"That's not important now," said Yasuke.

"Please, just take me to Yuki, take me to see my sister. You are honorable, Yasuke. I misjudged you," he confessed, his speech interrupted by the most burdened, painful coughs. "I distanced myself from Yuki after she gave birth to a foreign child, fearing Japan would never accept her. But you, Yasuke, have shown what true acceptance and honor mean."

Hideyoshi coughed loudly again, blood pouring from his mouth.

"Rest now; we'll be home soon," said Yasuke, rubbing Hideyoshi's back in a comforting gesture as they continued their somber journey.

As dusk settled over the village, Amara was pacing outside the house, her restlessness growing with the deepening shadows. The chill in the air seemed to echo her ever-mounting anxiety.

Inside, Yuki was also succumbing to apprehension; Yasuke's punctuality was as reliable as the sunrise, yet, with the day fading and supper long since cooled on the table, his absence was uncharacteristic and growing increasingly alarming.

Amara burst back inside with a sense of urgency that sliced through the tranquility of the home.

"Has he returned?" Yuki's voice wavered between hope and despair.

"No!" Amara responded, her eyes avoiding her mother's anxious gaze as she strode purposefully to her room. Moments later, she emerged, ambition on her face, katana glinting in her hand.

"I'm going to find him," she declared, her voice steady. "I cannot just sit here, waiting."

"I will join you," Chiyo called out, ready to act.

"No!" Yuki's voice was authoritative. "I will go with Amara. Girls, stay here in case he comes back."

Mother and daughter duly armed themselves and stepped into the encroaching darkness of the evening.

The world outside was now enveloped in night's embrace. As they descended the steps, a silhouette against the dark sky caught their attention—a tall figure moving slowly alongside a horse.

As they squinted into the darkness, they could make out a body slumped over the giant horse's back. They paused, mentally preparing to confront whatever lay ahead.

Amara adjusted the strap of her katana, her pulse racing with the anticipation of conflict, reminiscent of the skirmish they had endured just months before. But as the figure neared, a wave of relief washed over her and Yuki when they recognized the distinctive gait of the approaching silhouette. It was Yasuke coming toward them; he was wearied and staggering, but upright and alive.

That was all they needed to know.

The lantern Yuki held was issuing a soft, yellowish glow, revealing Yasuke's haggard face as he emerged from the blackness, his figure one of extreme fatigue.

Amara and Yuki hastened toward him, their relief quickly turning to concern as the lantern's light traced the contours of his bloodstained kimono, exposing sight of his wounds.

They halted abruptly when the slumped form on the horse came into view, its unresponsive appearance and the copious blood that stained the horse's flank sending a chill through the night.

"Yasuke!" Yuki's voice quivered with worry, her eyes brimming with unspoken questions. "What has happened? Where have you been? Who … who … is … this?"

Her voice trailed into a whisper, her heart sinking as she finally recognized the motionless body on the horse. There he was, her once estranged brother Hideyoshi, draped lifeless before her.

A storm of emotions churned within Yuki—sadness and empathy were drawn across her features, yet she steeled herself against the tears threatening to fall. She needed to know so much.

Yuki's gaze shifted back to Yasuke; her voice, a taut wire of bitterness and uncertainty, grappled with her assumptions. "Surely, he provided you with a worthy cause for your actions. Stubbornness was ever his blessing and his bane. Now, you have rightly slain him."

"No," Yasuke replied, his voice a heavy cloak of grief. "I did not do this to him. On my way back from Midoriya, I was accosted by three men seeking to press me into service under Lord Hideaki.

"I declined their offer, and violence ensued. These men were skilled … and just as I was losing ground, Hideyoshi intervened, granting me a crucial opportunity to regain composure. But by the time I could assist him, it was too late."

At these words, Yuki trembled visibly, her mind reeling as she struggled to comprehend Hideyoshi's reemergence back in Suruga and the dire consequences of his return. Even more so, she could not understand why he would have come to Yasuke's aid in such a way.

In the hush that followed, burdened by a heavy stillness, Yasuke, burdened by fatigue, led the horse bearing the slain Hideyoshi into the stable. With deliberate steps, Yuki and Amara accompanied him, their hands brushing the coarse texture of the hay.

Yasuke, with utmost care, lifted Hideyoshi from the horse and gently laid him down upon a makeshift hay bed.

"Amara, would you fetch some blankets?" Yasuke's request cut softly through the silence.

Without hesitation, Amara left to gather what was needed, returning swiftly to tuck the blankets around Hideyoshi's still form.

Yasuke then turned to Yuki, and within his gaze, a storm of sorrow mingled with enduring affection. He drew her close with an embrace bridging the gap between loss and love. In the refuge of Yasuke's arms, Yuki found herself transported back to the night of their fateful meeting, a night that seemed to span several lifetimes.

In that embrace, Yasuke felt the swell of Yuki's emotions, a tempestuous ocean wrought by the storied past with her brother.

The siblings' tumultuous bond had driven itself into Yuki's very soul. On this sad night, Yasuke bore a message that weighed heavily on his heart. "Hideyoshi wished for your presence at his end," Yasuke said solemnly, his words softly sounding in the stable. "Yet the road was too long, and his strength too fleeting. In his final lucid moments, he entrusted me to transcribe his last words for you."

Delicately, Yasuke retrieved a folded letter from within his garment, the parchment's edges crumpled by the journey.

Yuki's hands trembled as she took hold of the thin message, her pulse thrumming with dread and longing.

Each beat of her heart was a drumbeat to sound the final chapter of Hideyoshi's life—a chapter that lay unopened in her hands. Yet, she could not bring herself to open it. Not at this moment.

Yuki bowed her head, enveloped in the deep silence of the stable.

"Hideyoshi uttered fair words for me too," said Yasuke quietly. "Against all odds, he respected me at the end. Even before the end. And I respected him too; we were no longer enemies."

Yuki simply narrowed her eyes, then said, "I don't understand."

A solemn tranquility permeated the air, acknowledging the loss of Yuki's last direct family member. Compelled by a need for reflection, she stepped outside into the crisp night air, where her breath mingled with the cold, draping misty veils across a frosty, starlit sky.

Memories of her childhood surged forward—years overshadowed by the stern criticisms of Hideyoshi and their father, especially after their mother's premature death from illness.

Yuki remembered the oppressive expectations to conform to traditional roles, starkly contrasting her innate free spirit, often the target of harsh verbal reprimands and a harsh emotional toll.

With a sad heart, Yuki re-entered the stable, meeting Yasuke's gaze, her eyes laden with sorrow. Redirecting her focus, she addressed the immediate needs. "We should begin planning his funeral rites," she said, her voice gaining some steadiness in the act of planning, something she excelled at. "Hideyoshi didn't value faith as Mother and I did, never embracing Buddhism. Given the life he led, I feel his spirit must be freed from earthly bounds to avert further anguish."

"I will see to the arrangements for a cremation first thing tomorrow," Yasuke assured her, his touch comforting as he held her hand. "However, the man who helped me tonight was not the Hideyoshi we knew. He was changed, seeking atonement. The man you remember was gone. I know it is hard to believe ..."

Yasuke then gently kissed her hand. "Yuki, do what you do so excellently. Forgive him for the past," he implored. "In his last moments, I swear he was transformed. Despite knowing his limits in combat, he intervened, fully aware of the possible consequences. He came to save me, Yuki. Let us acknowledge that."

"Perhaps you're right," Yuki conceded, her emotions tangled as she let out a deep sigh. "Though that's my brother lying there, it feels like he belonged to another life, one far removed from the present."

She lingered, staring at Hideyoshi's lifeless form, lost in thought.

After a moment, Yasuke gently guided her away, and back inside.

That night, neither Yasuke nor Yuki could find peace.

As dawn broke, signaling a new day, birds chirped, and morning dew glistened on the grass. Yasuke, though still so weary from the ordeal, prepared a bucket of water and a rag and headed back to the stable where Hideyoshi's body lay. He was ready to begin the respectful preparations for his final rites.

Yasuke, his muscles aching, and his body exhausted from the prior day's struggles, carefully lifted Hideyoshi's lifeless form onto a large cart typically used for hauling bales of hay.

He adjusted the body to ensure it was stable and seated in a respectful stance, then searched the barn for materials to secure it.

Methodically, Yasuke started the solemn task of preparing Hideyoshi for cremation, removing the bloodstained and dirtied garments in accordance with the funeral rites.

He began by gently washing Hideyoshi's feet, each movement deliberate and laden with respect. As he worked, Yuki entered the stable, nodding to Yasuke in a solemn greeting to mark the morning.

"Are you faring well today?" Yuki inquired, her voice low and steady.

"Pain and fatigue course through me like the endless flow of a river," Yasuke responded, grimacing slightly.

He gently soaked the cloth and continued his task.

Yuki reached out, placing her hand on Yasuke's arm.

"Let me finish cleaning him," she offered softly.

Yasuke paused, noticing that Yuki avoided meeting his gaze as she had before. Sensing her distress, he probed, "Is everything all right?"

Yuki bowed her head, maintaining her avoidance of eye contact.

"Yes, everything is fine," she replied, barely above a whisper.

"This isn't the truth," Yasuke pressed. "You are burdened, yet you seem distant."

Slowly, Yuki lifted her eyes to meet his, her expression unreadable. "I spent last night haunted by our conversation, wondering if being more like a traditional Japanese woman might have saved Hideyoshi."

She paused, the conflict written clearly across her face.

"I've been reflecting on my entire life, and I've come to realize that perhaps I need to embrace the traditional ways more fully to protect what remains of our family. It has taken me this long to see it."

Yuki's words lingered, her declaration marking a poignant moment of self-reckoning and a deep, personal unease.

Yasuke said, "No matter how deeply we reflect, we cannot change the past. The person we believe we project to the world is different from how the world truly sees us. Are you content with your family?"

Yuki remained silent, her gaze fixed on the dimly lit stable floor.

Yasuke stepped closer, his voice warm. "Each member of this family is here because of who you are, and who you are not.

"A traditional Japanese woman did not bring this family into your life. She did not bring me to you. She would never have brought me."

He paused briefly, his eyes searching hers. "We are all here together because you are not a traditional Japanese woman. Thus, the good in your life outweighs the bad. I see nothing but good in you."

Yuki looked down, her eyes reflecting the slow demise of a faintly flickering light. "Perhaps the world sees more clearly than I do."

Yasuke inclined his head.

"The world sees only shadows and light. Yet in between lies the truth of who we are."

Yuki slowly nodded, finally meeting Yasuke's gaze.

"Then I shall hold my family close and cast away the shadows."

A quiet smile touched Yasuke's lips. "In this way, the light within you will continue to shine."

Yuki inhaled deeply, Yasuke's words penetrating her soul, offering solace. "You're right; I'm sorry I let my thoughts wander too far. I … I will continue my work here with Hideyoshi."

Yasuke nodded in acknowledgment. "I will go to the temple and ensure there's space and time available for Hideyoshi soon."

"Thank you," Yuki said as he headed to the horse, her gratitude apparent. As he mounted his horse and rode off, she turned back to Hideyoshi's body and continued the meticulous cleansing, her movements now steadier and her will as unflinching as ever.

Yuki had taken Yasuke's comforting words to heart, channeling her focus into the meticulous preparation of Hideyoshi's body. It was more than a task for her; it was a way to channel her grief and find closure. By the time Yasuke returned to the stable, she had completed her solemn duties. Hideyoshi was dressed in his shini-shōzoku, the traditional funeral garments, his appearance serene and dignified.

He lay in a pure white kimono, signifying mourning and purity, with a loosely tied obi belt around his waist and white tabi socks on his feet. Yasuke paused at the entrance, taken aback by the careful arrangement and the peaceful aura it conveyed.

After observing silently, Yasuke walked through the garden searching for Yuki. He found her with Sakura among the blossoms, both tending to the flowers.

"Your brother's attire was applied with the precision of a sound mind," Yasuke remarked, reflecting a great respect for her efforts.

"I am pleased to receive your compliment," Yuki responded, not looking up. "Were you able to make arrangements at the temple?"

"Yes, after some convincing, they agreed to perform his final rites tomorrow afternoon. Are you mentally prepared for it? Perhaps you should allow a few more days to grieve. I realize you feel it's unnecessary, but maybe it's what you need to confront the past."

"That will not be needed," Yuki replied firmly, her tone leaving no room for argument as her eyes remained fixed on the garden.

Five monks, clad in their somber black robes, arrived before dawn on the following day to collect Hideyoshi's body.

They took turns rewashing Hideyoshi with their purified water to ensure the Buddhist customs were adhered to.

An eerie silence enveloped the temple grounds, broken only when the lead monk initiated his harmonious chant, soon joined in unison by the others. The air filled with the rhythmic, melodious recitation of sutras, creating a solemn atmosphere as they placed Hideyoshi onto a pyre made of fragrant cypress wood.

All the girls stood by Yuki, offering silent support, their expressions somber as they exchanged glances.

As the ceremony progressed, the eldest monk took a torch engulfed in flames and moved gingerly toward the pyre.

At that moment, Yuki, overcome by emotion, suddenly rose, scurrying a short distance away from the gathering. Yasuke and the girls held back, aware that Yuki needed this moment alone to confront what she had been avoiding for so long.

The monk with the torch paused, sensing the shift in mood.

Yasuke caught his eye and nodded, signaling him to continue.

Alone, tears beginning to fill her eyes, Yuki reached into her kimono and pulled out the letter Yasuke had lovingly transcribed from Hideyoshi's final words. The bloodstains on it seemed to ignite the turmoil within her even further.

The chants grew louder as the eldest monk lit the pyre, setting Hideyoshi's body ablaze.

Surrounded by the sound of crackling wood and resonant chants, Yuki unfolded the letter. Tears streamed down her cheeks, spattering onto the paper, the words blurring under her immense grief.

Yuki,

As the twilight of my life hastens its approach, my thoughts, heavy with remorse, turn toward you. The paths I walked, governed by rigid beliefs and a heart sealed from the world's diverse drapery, have led us down a road of estrangement. My resistance to the unfamiliar has bred naught but sorrow for us and widened the gap between our hearts.

Since our mother's untimely departure, the sands of change have relentlessly shifted, molding my perceptions in an unfortunate light.

In my youth, your spirited demeanor seemed a divergence from our esteemed traditions—a breeze too wild for the tranquil gardens of our ancestors. Yet, as the end of my days nears, I perceive in you our mother's indomitable essence.

Her unconventional ways were the very sinew that fortified our lineage, crafting a legacy not of conformity but of resilience and uniqueness.

It is with profound regret that I acknowledge how my own fears and pride obscured the beauty and vigor of your independence. In these waning moments, I contemplate the warmth and acceptance I withheld, which you rightly deserved.

As I prepare to rejoin the earth, I entrust these words to you, hoping they may mend the rift wrought by my errors. May you find the compassion to forgive a lost brother whose eyes opened far too late.

With a heart now unshackled yet burdened with regret, I offer you my heartfelt and humble apologies.

With enduring affection,

Hideyoshi.

Yuki's hands trembled as she carefully folded the letter, tucking it away again within her kimono.

"I forgive you ... I forgive you," she murmured aloud, tears coursing down her cheeks. The silence that enveloped her was a stark contrast to the intensifying crackle of the pyre. In that moment, Yuki found herself traversing the long-suppressed corridors of her pain, finally opening the gates to her present and future.

Since her mother's death, she had staunchly withheld all her tears, remaining dry-eyed even at her father's passing. Yet, Hideyoshi's words had kindled a spark of hope, not just for her family but for all the women of Japan who dared to defy its societal expectations.

Amara, with her mixed heritage, epitomized such defiance.

More likely to wield a sword than a serving tray, she symbolized the great potential of a revolutionary era.

Forgiving Hideyoshi marked a crucial step toward embracing this new era, setting the stage for a much-needed societal and political transformation.

As the final rites unfolded and Yuki returned to the gathering, the blazing pyre helped dry out her tears, the heat warming her face.

A rosy glow had kissed each of her cheeks.

Amara approached, her smile also a beacon of comfort.

"If I may say so, Okāsan, you seem at peace," she observed.

"I am," Yuki responded almost in a whisper.

Amara squeezed her mother's hand.

"Good, because I sense a change brewing, and you are the cornerstone of our home. We need your strength more than ever."

"No," Yuki remonstrated. "The true cornerstone is your father, Yasuke."

Amara shook her head slightly. " Okāsan, it is your resilience that fortifies us all. You maintain the harmony allowing us each to thrive. chichi-ue protects us, but you … You nurture and sustain our spirits."

"You're wise beyond your years, my beautiful daughter," Yuki said, stroking Amara's hair. I, too, worry that the changes ahead may not be gentle. We must be strong, patient, and united, for the coming years will undoubtedly test our steadfastness and defenses."

Yasuke and the other girls started heading toward them, hoping to join in a collective embrace.

Amara gazed at her family against the backdrop of the roaring flames, her eyes alight with the reflection of the fire. Determined, she added, "We may not appear intimidating, Okāsan, but beneath our calm exterior, we harbor a strength forged in the fires of adversity. Together, there is nothing we cannot withstand."

Yuki shared Amara's sentiment as they watched the fire's elemental dance reflect the inevitable transformation of their lives and spirits.